MIRROR ME

A Mirror Novel

STEPHANIE TYLER

MIRROR ME

A MIRROR NOVEL

Kayla Peters hasn't been Claire Cooper for six years…but the past is about to catch up with her, and nothing will ever be the same.

Kayla's in witness protection, being hidden from her twin sister by the US Marshals Office. When Kayla moves in next to a former Special Forces operative, she discovers that he's got a dark, dangerous past of his own…and that he might be the only person who can help her survive.

Teige doesn't want to like Kayla. Since the death of his CO and Teige's retirement from Delta Force, he's been taking on the most dangerous jobs, pressing the luck he feels has followed him his entire life. He's convinced it'll run out, because he knows no one can be that lucky all the time. And when he discovers who Kayla really is, and what kind of trouble's following her, he realizes he's up against the most dangerous—and personal—job of his career.

The belief in a supernatural source of evil is not necessary; men alone are quite capable of every wickedness.
—"Under Western Eyes" by Joseph Conrad

Whatever I see I swallow immediately.
—"Mirror" by Sylvia Plath

Prologue

SHE CAN'T SCREAM. She *must be* screaming inside her head, but her throat's too tight for sound. Her body's heavy, her limbs weighed down like she's been drugged.

Later, she'll discover it had merely been fear rendering her unable to move or yell. They'll find claw marks in the oak floor, where she'd been digging in with her fingernails, attempting to drag her frozen body across the floor—and toward the scene, not away from it.

Anyone who knows her won't be surprised.

But right now, she's trapped, watching the extreme happenings not more than ten feet from her. She blinks hard, tells herself she's dreaming even though she's painfully aware of how real all of it is.

They've always known it would come to this, even after taking steps for years to prevent it. All of those preparations are proven useless tonight.

His screams hurt her ears, but she wouldn't cover them even if she could. She has to be strong any way she can.

It's a genuine horror show. No movie could ever get this right—the blood spatter, the unmistakable metallic scent, the anguished cries...they're beyond human.

Everyone becomes a beast when they die. Everyone begs. She knows that now. And she will never, ever forget what she's borne witness to. It's irrevocable, and it's more than a memory.

It's a nightmare she might never wake from.

But she's not the one being hurt and she tries to yell, "Stop," tries to say something, anything that might make it all end, but nothing comes out but a too-soft whimper. It's followed by a dying man's tortured screams.

There's a burst of fire that incites a new terror in her. It's her turn. She scrabbles on the floor, exhausting herself with the effort. She hears soft laughter and sees that she's in the same exact spot, that she hasn't moved even an inch. The blood that began to seep toward her stops, the controlled fire burning away the flesh and bone and finally his screams have stopped.

But it's not over. Her head throbs, her tongue hangs uselessly and her throat burns from the smoke and her choking tears so that she can barely breathe.

The sound of a siren's burst breaking through her terror is the only thing that stops her from being the next victim, but she won't know that until hours later when she's conscious. She'll wake in the hospital, screaming out loud this time, and she'll see familiar faces.

She'll know it wasn't a dream or a nightmare. She'll remember that his limbs were sawed off and he lived through it. That he was still technically alive when the fire began to burn him.

She'll want to ask, "Did he feel it?" but won't. Because she knows the answer and doesn't want to hear them lie. They would do it out of kindness, but there's no room for that here. She's been taught that there's a time and a place for everything, but the rules have changed.

She realizes there was never any room for rules in the first place.

Chapter 1

16 years later
Colombia, South America

Master Sergeant Teige Junos lay belly down in the thick grass, camouflaged from predators. As the hours passed, his breathing had slowed and he'd stopped sweating. How much longer he could remain unmoving in the blazing temperatures was a testament to his training.

But this wasn't training, and he wasn't alone.

Next to him, his CO, Sergeant Major Greg MacDonald, lay in the same position. They'd been there for over twenty-four hours, staring through the murky waves of heat, when the sudden roar of enemy gunfire slammed through the still air overhead. Without a word between them, both began a commando crawl that was more like a swim through the wet jungle floor's humidity.

They finally found shelter about half a mile away, a ditch that afforded them some respite from the unexpected blasts. They dug in, not returning fire in hopes that not drawing attention to themselves would make the conflict end sooner.

Hunched down, covered in sweat, Teige watched the explosions erupting in the sky like blazes of glory. The scent of gunfire mingled with the unmistakable smell of blood and death, the air vibrating with the disturbance.

The recon that began peacefully had caught him and Mac in the middle of two warring factions in the outskirts of Bogota. Definitely a wrong place, wrong time situation.

"Maybe they'll all just kill each other," Mac murmured.

Teige hoped they'd be that lucky, even as he kept his M16 at the ready. He and Mac could take on a big group alone, if necessary, but being Delta Force was about being smart. You risked when you were forced to risk. And this wasn't their fight.

Hours before, during the monotony of the recon, Mac broke their silence to tell Teige he was retiring. That his wife was tired after twenty years of secrets and lies.

"Big step, Mac."

"It won't be easy leaving all this," he'd said with only the barest trace of sarcasm and a genuine smile. "But she hung around this long—I owe her."

Teige had smiled too, because that was pretty much why he never got too involved in relationships. At least that's what he told himself.

As of now, there was no one even remotely special at home. He'd ended things with Diane for the hundredth time because it was never going to work. They both knew it but were drawn to each other like magnets. Or bad pennies.

"You'll find her," Mac had said in response to Teige's silence.

"I'm old enough not to worry about it," Teige had told Mac honestly. He could stay in Delta Force in several different capacities for twenty more years, if he got lucky.

If he remained lucky.

"You don't have to—it'll happen. One day, she's going to show up and you're just gonna know. That's how it happens for guys like us—it's like lightning. None of this 'she might be the one' shit. You see her, and you're going to want to go caveman and throw her over your shoulder and that's the end of that shit."

Teige had tried to imagine Mac's wife responding to that and he'd laughed.

"Keep laughing, boy. You know I'm always right." Mac was always right. It was why Teige listened when Mac urged, "Curl up," as a long bout of gunfire rang out overhead.

A few shells landed in the hole with them, one close enough to burn the hell out of his ear, and he kept his head down. It seemed like forever and then there was a sudden quiet, which was a more deadly sound than the shooting.

His ears rang and he fought the urge to peer out. When he finally did, he'd expected to see a lot of dead men left to rot.

He looked over at Mac, murmured, "Shit, that was close."

Mac didn't answer. The bullet had gone clean through the front of his skull, a lucky shot that had nothing at all to do with skill.

After two more hours of quiet, Teige was still stunned as he dragged himself up and hoisted Mac's body over his shoulder. He walked over the bodies and out of the jungle toward the waiting helo five klicks away, even as daylight turned to dusk. And amazingly enough, he didn't run across any soldiers.

Lucky, the doc had told him.

Teige had been lucky before, had watched someone he loved slowly kill himself for years before finally dying. Teige had been lucky not to have been there the night it happened, but his sister had been. It was pure luck that she'd survived.

One of these days, all that luck was going to kill him.

Chapter 2

Three years later

Kayla could live here forever, she decided, and she hadn't said that about any of the last four places she'd lived, or the three before that, or the earliest ones, which were a blur of bad carpets and ugly bedspreads.

But this, the old blue Victorian with a rambling porch and a wild yard...this seemed like heaven.

"You look familiar," Mrs. Mueller told her.

Kayla had just cut bangs, wore glasses she didn't need and still, she'd never escape that statement. "I have one of those faces," she murmured.

"Are you working in the area?" Mrs. Mueller asked.

"I'm a freelance photographer. I can pay the first two months and security in cash," Kayla assured her while side-stepping the question.

Mrs. Mueller looked like she was going to press her on that but instead changed tactics, asking, "Are you married?"

"No."

"Well, you're young yet."

"Twenty-five," Kayla agreed.

"Where's your family, dear?"

Normally, Kayla would've found the questions intrusive, but Mrs. Mueller had a disarming way about her. She also had kind eyes and a no-nonsense approach that suited her as well as her short dark hair and simple sweatsuit. "My parents are dead."

She heard Abby—her new marshal's—voice in her head. *Keep your story as close to the truth as possible. Make it consistent and simple.*

Mrs. Mueller patted her on the shoulder. "Now that my own kids are grown and moved away, I like to think of my renters as my kids."

Mrs. Muller owned the three houses in this small enclave, and they were the only houses on this very private block where two of the houses, including the one Kayla wanted to rent, backed up to the woods, which made her almost not take it. But when she toured the house, she couldn't say no.

The man who lived next door was a retired soldier, a *very nice man*, Mrs. Mueller explained. She'd been renting to him for fifteen years and he was always helpful. *When he's around.* Mrs. Mueller herself spent summers in New York with her daughter and grandkids, winters here, so she was gone for months at a time.

That meant Kayla would be completely alone. But all

she had to do was make sure she had a working truck and cell service. She had both, so her decision was made. "I'd like to move in as soon as possible."

"Give me a check and you can move in tonight." Mrs. Mueller's eyes sparkled. "I think you're going to find the peace you're looking for here."

Kayla must've looked startled, because Mrs. Mueller patted her arm reassuringly. "I knew you were coming, because the tarot cards I read every morning told me."

Tarot cards.

"I'll do a reading for you when you're all settled in," Mrs. Mueller continued. "Go on now, looks like rain."

Kayla watched her new landlady walk across the lawn with her cane held in the air, and smiled a little.

Tarot cards. She supposed there were odder things in life. Certainly it seemed like a harmless hobby, although Kayla didn't like anyone looking into her life, no matter if it was a detective or a crystal ball.

But the marshals had checked out Mrs. Mueller and the neighborhood and they'd given Kayla the okay to stay here. She hoped it would be for a nice long while, since she'd spent months bumping around the country in bad motel rooms in order to throw off anyone tracking her.

Her new handler assured Kayla that she'd succeeded. Kayla wasn't as sure, but she couldn't live out of any more suitcases. She needed a home and 12 Wildwood Drive was it.

As she started to pull her things out of the truck she'd purchased in Georgia four months earlier, she heard Mrs.

Mueller call, "The diner up the road has good food. Better company."

Kayla turned toward Mrs. Mueller, but she'd already gone inside her own house. Kayla nodded as if Mrs. Mueller could see her anyway. And then she got to work.

She'd just finished hauling the last of her belongings from the truck to the porch—admittedly, not all that much —when the rain started. It pattered the ground with fat drops that sounded like marbles falling on stone, and steam rose from the hot pavement.

The front door was unlocked and she had the two sets of keys in her pocket. A waft of warm air hit her when she opened the door. There were A/Cs for most rooms and she turned all of them on, plus the ceiling fans, before dragging her things inside the front hallway. When she finished, she gave a final glance outside, locked the door and slid the deadbolt into place with a reassuring click. And then she began to walk around the house, checking things out again.

It was clean and freshly painted, waiting for its new occupant.

"I'm it," she said out loud on the third floor and got a creak in response.

She wheeled around and saw nothing. Wanted to laugh at herself for being so jumpy but she couldn't. She checked everywhere but found nothing that would've made the creak.

Just the house settling, she told herself firmly.

And then she heard the creaking again, just before she felt the chill, like something cold touched her arm. She smelled a sharp, spicy cologne and then nothing.

Tarot cards and ghosts. Mrs. Mueller hadn't mentioned anything about the house being haunted, but Kayla liked that better than the alternative.

It wouldn't have mattered, not after Kayla had seen the back bedroom on the third floor that was actually inside the turret of the house. It wasn't the biggest room, but it had the best view of the woods behind the house.

She would always be scared of the darkness surrounding her, but something about this place made her feel like she could face the night for the first time in years.

———

Her new renter was running from something, Willa Mueller mused as she spread the tarot cards on the old mahogany table in front of her, and Sommersville, North Carolina was as good place to end up as any. She and Walt had lived here from the time they'd gotten married, with Walt commuting to the Post, because she'd wanted to be an independent Army wife. She'd always been different, held her ground. And Walt liked coming home to a place that wasn't in the middle of a military town.

Now this town had become something of a haven for retired military folks and their families. It was familiar. Quaint.

Kayla was too thin, Willa decided. The young woman needed plenty of good meals, good sleep and good friends. Those three things could heal you like nothing else.

Despite the dark circles, Kayla was pretty, with the dark ponytail contrasting the blue of her eyes and those cute freckles sprinkled across her nose. Her daughter Joanie had those same freckles. Kayla would always look younger than she was.

She was also haunted. And Willa Mueller knew haunted.

Chapter 3

THE THIRD FLOOR was a good choice for her bedroom, Kayla decided, bypassing the larger master bedroom on the second floor. She'd rigged both sets of stairs and had the portable escape ladder that she could use to lower herself to the back porch, just in case.

There was plenty of time to run for safety if there was a break-in. There was also a .38 Special she carried with her at all times.

Weapon in hand, she walked around, lighting every room in the house. There were already plain white cotton sheets hung over the old curtain rods on all the windows, care of Mrs. Mueller.

The sheets were clean but worn, which was good. She could see shadows through them.

Finally, she went upstairs and settled in on the double mattress shoved in the corner—it was on a box spring, which was directly on the floor. No worrying about anyone hiding under the bed. She climbed under the sheet and put what she needed within reach. Beyond the gun, she had a flashlight and a knife. She also had her Kindle, and the small TV was turned on, volume low, and placed on the dresser across the room.

She'd set up the cameras the way Hoss had taught her. He'd been so good about helping her learn how to secure her surroundings.

From her bed, she could peek out two windows. There was a single light on at Mrs. Mueller's. None at the house next door. She hadn't seen a car come or go from there all day.

The hypervigilance she embraced like a religion came with a cost—exhaustion from staying up all night and trying to sleep during the day—but it was one she'd gladly pay.

In the beginning, there had been prescriptions to make her sleep, to soothe her anxiety. But they'd made it worse. Being in control of her body calmed her more than anything, and vigilance wasn't so bad. Soldiers, the FBI, police and marshals practiced it.

But you're just a civilian.

No, not *just*. She'd seen far too much to be considered just anything.

The creaks started again down the small hallway that connected the two rooms.

"You don't scare me," she called out. "I have plenty of my own ghosts."

There was no answer, but the creaking stopped.

While Kayla sat at the ready, Teige was sitting on his back porch, couched in darkness. Learning to see well in the dark was, to some extent, an acquired skill that demanded equal parts patience and constant training. The only thing throwing it off was the blazing lights from the house next door.

Willa Mueller left him the message about *the nice, young single woman* who'd rented it.

He'd laughed in spite of himself, then called Mac a bastard from beyond the grave.

He'd been back from some shithole for two days, holed up inside the house during the day. Decompressing used to be mandated for his Delta Force team whenever they'd come home from a mission. The operatives would house together on Post in seclusion, supposedly for the purposes of debriefing. Really it gave the psychologists a chance to assess them, and the docs a chance to make sure everything was medically okay. It gave the men a chance to come back down from the mission before they saw their families—and everything else—that invaded once real life hit.

Soldiers just back from war were in no way ready for real life, and real life sure as hell wasn't ready for them.

Now he had to provide his own form of forced seclusion. Sometimes he stayed at a hotel so he didn't feel guilty about ducking Willa, although she typically understood soldiers. He was pretty sure she was aware he'd been Delta, but Delta seemed a long time ago. At least until nights like this, with sticky wet air mimicking the jungles, soaking his skin.

He was shirtless, running sneakers still on, his chest

heaving less than it had been ten minutes earlier. Ten miles and it still wasn't enough. He could've kept going, pushing his muscles to the limit. He'd been in the zone and then the images flashed through his mind and he'd stopped dead.

Hanny was the only one who could handle his moods these days, but he hadn't picked her up from the dog sitter yet, because that would mean seeing people. Interacting.

Tomorrow was better.

He flexed up on his toes to stretch out his calves before diving back into the woods. Ten more miles should do it. Ten more miles would bring the dawn, and maybe even sleep.

He laughed out loud again, figuring that had to be some kind of record.

Chapter 4

KAYLA WAS on the witness stand, boxed in, the microphone in front of her. She stared out into the sea of faces but couldn't focus on any one of them.

"Do you swear to tell the truth, the whole truth and nothing but the truth, so help you God?"

She raised her right hand. "I do."

The gavel came down hard enough to make her jump. She opened her mouth to ask a question, but when she looked out at the courtroom, the only person she saw was herself, staring back at her, telling her, "I'll always be with you."

She woke with a short scream, halting it quickly, hoping no one in the neighborhood heard anything. The air conditioners should've blocked the noise, she hoped as she put a hand to her heart. It hammered a tattoo against her chest and her breathing was too fast.

She'd known, between the drive and the move, that she wouldn't be able to stay up all night. Normally she would, sleeping during the day instead. Nightmares when it was light out somehow weren't as bad, but now it was pitch black and she was shaking.

"Dammit," she muttered. A creak down the hall answered her. "I'm okay."

The roll of thunder rumbled around the house. She did a swift check of the cameras and saw everything was fine inside the house. Outside too. No one was moving around, no cars—just swaying trees and lightning tearing up the sky.

She pulled on a sweatshirt and went to look out the windows into the backyard.

The storm was escalating. Taking pictures from inside the house wouldn't be nearly as satisfying. Going outside on a night like this was crazy, but she'd learned to trust in the unpredictability of a storm. Because during the height of the madness had never required her to practice the ultimate caution. It was the calm days, the ones where it seemed as if nothing bad could possibly happen, that made her nervous, caught her off guard. Made her think that things were fine.

Storms didn't hide what they were. They couldn't pretend they were anything but bent on total and utter destruction, no matter their path. She'd learned to appreciate things like that. The rain was a comfortable blanket of nature's wrath that could shield her from everyone and everything.

Storms were safe, and this one raged around her house.

In response, she threw on a baseball hat and pushed the back door open against the wind to stand on the porch with her camera in hand. She'd switched to digital mostly, like the rest of the world, but she missed the feel of real film and the darkroom, that slow reveal of the pictures in the solution.

She began capturing the way the lightning ripped the sky open, rain showering right in front of the lens.

Beautiful. Ferocious. The world through the camera wasn't removed, but she was protected. She could see everything, but she went largely unnoticed as she lost track of time.

The sun would never break through the black clouds hovering. She edged the lens down, focused tightly on the line between the treetops and the horizon until something caught her eye. She edged downward, taking scads of pictures as she moved lower, but there was nothing. She zoomed in more tightly and that's when she spotted him.

It took everything she had not to put the camera down and walk away. But she comforted herself that the storm hid her as well as he'd been. And he wasn't even looking in her direction.

He blended in with the foliage and the storm without even trying. He remained unmoving, part of nature, part of the storm, like he'd been born from it.

She snapped over and over, needing to capture him, wild, feral, part of nature. And then he moved over to the woodpile in the clearing.

The soldier. Had to be.

The lightning tore through the sky, and the soldier chopping the large round logs either didn't notice or didn't care. It had to be the latter, she thought as he raised the ax to the sky like he was purposely taunting the electrical currents to come out and play. She snapped several pictures in a long string, the whirr of the camera lost in the sounds of the storm, the lightning mimicking a flash.

She blinked, and he was gone. She moved the camera away from her face and looked toward the soldier. Had she imagined him?

No, she thought as she went through his pictures on the camera, until a touch on the back of her biceps made her whirl around with a small scream. She nearly dropped the camera but she was aided by a large hand that cradled both wrists—and saved the hardware.

Him. Rain soaked. Angry.

He'd noticed her, all right.

"Why are you taking pictures of me?" he demanded, his voice a harsh growl. Up close, he was big. He wore no shirt, his chest muddied and scratched.

It took her what seemed like hours to answer, because her throat was dry and her heart thudded loudly in her ears. A tremble went through her, and really the only thing holding her up was sheer will and his hand on her arm. "You were in my shot," she managed finally.

"Delete. Them." His tone was a command.

"No." She held tight to the camera. *Very nice man,* my ass.

"You can't take pictures of me like that—not without my express permission and I'm not giving it. So delete them."

"I'm not...they're for me."

"And who the hell are you that you need pictures of me?"

Excellent question. "Who the hell are you?" she shot back and he froze.

Christ, Teige, hold it together. You're scaring the shit out of her.

She was five foot four at most. Baseball cap pulled all the way down, the bill casting a shadow even when she raised her head to see him.

Blue eyes the color of the warm ocean flashed at him. Bowed mouth. Baggy sweats, bare feet. Young. Innocent, maybe, but her eyes reminded him of the expression his mother used to use—*She's got an old soul.*

He didn't even want to know her name.

He didn't answer her question either, telling her instead, "You can't take pictures of soldiers like that. It's a safety measure." He might not still be a soldier but there was a price on his head in several countries he knew about and probably more he didn't.

Finally, she took a breath. "Okay, yes, sure—I get that." She held the camera's viewfinder so he could see it. "Do you want any copies before I delete them?"

He stared at the picture like he was looking at a stranger. "No, just delete them."

She did, one by one, showed him that she only had pictures left of the trees and the sky. When she got to the end, she looked up at him.

He was gone.

But he wasn't completely erased from her camera. Nothing was gone permanently in the digital age, not the way he would've liked. She went inside, locked the door and went to work retrieving the deletions from her memory card.

She felt guilty, like she'd violated his privacy in a way—and she hated not respecting that. She deleted all of them except the one that she printed out to keep. She couldn't bring herself to destroy it. It was so perfect. He looked beautiful. Ethereal. Like he belonged to the earth and the sky, like a God summoning the thunder.

She put it in the desk drawer and closed it.

The rain had stopped. The sun began to come through the trees. Another day.

Teige had been watching her through the trees for ten minutes before she'd slid her lens in his direction and started snapping. She hadn't seen him immediately, but when she had, he felt it as sharp as a knife.

Despite the rain and the rumble of thunder, he'd heard her footsteps, the whir of the camera as sharp as helo blades.

And you're back in the jungle again.

For a brief second, he'd flashed back to that day, that specific damned mission that ruined him worse than any of the others, even the ones he'd taken heavy losses on. He didn't know how he pulled himself back, since the greenery in the backyard looked as thick and heavy as any jungle in any godforsaken part of the world.

But it wasn't. Not the place where Mac got his head

blown off. It was his backyard, and his stress level was through the roof.

Fuck PTSD. He'd worked through that shit. Been working steadily through it for years. Today would be no different.

Work would be the thing to heal him. Work and nothing more. He forced himself to forget about the girl and her camera and the fact that she was living next door. Those pictures she took were so painfully personal, even he could see it.

He looked wild, his teeth bared as if trying to exorcize all the devils from all the jungles he'd waded into. She'd captured the way he felt inside.

How the hell had she done that?

There were landmines everywhere. It didn't matter where in the hell he stepped. Staying away rather than figuring out why would be the challenge.

You'll have to apologize.

He brushed that thought aside in favor of standing outside, letting his body soak up the rain. Some whiskey would help him come down. And then he'd finally be able to goddamned sleep.

"Daniels, did you get your witness set up?"

US Marshal Abby Daniels leaned back in her chair to see her direct supervisor, Carl Lissner, coming down the hall toward her. She'd been at her desk for the majority of the evening, going over paperwork on her current cases.

Now, her neck was stiff, her right arm was killing her from spending too much time with the mouse, and she desperately needed more coffee. "Yes, alarm system in place. New IDs, bank accounts, the works."

Carl stopped in front of her desk, handed her a hot coffee she gratefully accepted. His face had that craggy handsomeness that still had a lot of the female marshals and support staff swooning over him. She knew the attention embarrassed him more than he'd admit.

He took a sip of his coffee. "It's been over six months since any sightings."

And that means jack shit. "All that means is that the FBI still can't find Mara. It doesn't mean Mara can't find her sister."

Finally, he sat down, their gazes level, like he was done treading lightly. "Kayla's most recent handler was killed."

"You told me that last month. What's your point?" She couldn't help but sound annoyed. She was one of the younger marshals, yes. Female, yes. Family history that might make this case difficult for her, yes. But this checking up on her shit wasn't something she'd expected from him.

His tone gentled when he told her, "You know exactly what my point is.

"I'm handling the new witness and myself."

"Any reason you put her in a house next to your brother?"

She shrugged and tried to look innocent. "It was empty."

"Daniels," he warned but she simply blinked. He gave

her a pained look and she nodded, message received. He got up and walked away.

She was nearly alone in the large office, save for security staff and the marshal on duty who was no doubt catching some sleep in the small room set aside for that purpose. There were several bunk beds, a shower and laundry facility in case an overnight—or several—were warranted.

She turned back to her file, played with the frayed envelope paper-clipped to the inside flap. The letter was at least eight months old, addressed to Hoss at his field office in Kansas and placed in Kayla's file.

She'd memorized the content already, written in painfully perfect script with a leaking black pen. And she'd never be able to forget it, no matter how hard she tried.

Daddy always used to say practice makes perfect.

The first one was practice and it felt perfect. I picked someone who deserved it. If they didn't, it wasn't fair and Daddy always said to play fair.

I was just doing what Daddy taught me. Claire did too... she's not innocent, like she claims. My sister's a murderer too. She just doesn't want to admit it.

Chapter 5

HE WAITED at the entrance of the park where the family picnic was being held. He only went because Roy begged him to, so he wouldn't be alone in the sea of families.

Teige knew that was bullshit. Roy loved the family shit and wanted Teige to find someone to love, same as Mac had wanted for him. If Roy thought a park filled with screaming kids and exhausted-looking parents would push Teige in that direction, the guy was crazier than Teige thought.

"Welcome to paradise," Roy said, a baby strapped to his chest and a toddler clinging to his hand. His wife, Lia, was behind them with the twin girls and Teige muttered something about birth control. "I hear you and I'm ignoring you."

He'd met Roy in the Rangers. They'd gone through Delta training together, but Roy had gotten out quickly once his wife got sick with breast cancer. She was recovering now, but Roy spent a lot of time with her and the kids. He had family money that allowed it, although he never acted like he was a rich kid.

They'd stayed close, Roy always being his main contact when Teige went on jobs. Roy was probably the only person on the planet who actually knew where Teige was at all times, a responsibility he handled well.

"Dude, seriously, glad you could make it," Roy told him.

"Thanks for the invite," he muttered, opening the gate for his friend. Hanny ran through first, and she didn't stop running. "Shit."

"She never does that," Roy said.

Teige whistled but was completely ignored by the German shepherd he'd inherited as a pup two years earlier. From Roy. The man would never admit he'd brought the dog home on purpose because he'd known Lia wouldn't let him keep it. That same night, he'd looked as forlorn as Hanny when he'd knocked on Teige's door. Teige had trained her, grown to love the big beast more than he'd admit.

There was, of course, some screaming as the giant dog —which looked more like a wolf—ran through the crowded park, but most recognized her. He hightailed it through the clusters of people and caught up to Hanny as she was running toward a woman. Her hair was long and dark, pulled back in a loose ponytail, and she turned because people were pointing at the monster bearing down on her.

She stared for a split second, then smiled, like Hanny was the best thing she'd ever seen. She bent down and clapped her hands but she hadn't needed to. Hanny was on her like a heat-seeking missile.

The woman wore a vintage AC/DC T-shirt and jeans.

The woman made his heart nearly goddamned stop.

It was *her*. There was no rain this time, but the palpable tension still vibrated between them, zinging through him like an electric shock and threatening to explode.

The dog stopped as soon as it got in front of Kayla, and then it sat, patiently.

"Hey, aren't you beautiful," she told it, held out her palm and got the quick lick of approval. Then she patted its neck for distraction while she gingerly checked the tags with her free hand.

"Hanny," she said and got an openmouthed pant of approval. The tag listed Teige Junos as the owner, along with a phone number, and she pulled her cell phone out to call him.

Before she could dial, a red-faced man came up fast next to her. For a quick second she thought it was the dog's owner, until he started yelling at her. "Your dog needs to be on a leash, dammit."

"She's not my dog," Kayla started, but the man continued.

"I don't know who you think you are, but you're not following the rules and I'm going to report you."

The anger rose fast and hot for her, and she attempted

to swallow it back. But the man kept yelling and she stood, ready to yell back. Before she could say anything, a low male voice that sent a tingle up her spine said, "It's my dog, so why don't you yell at me?"

Kayla looked up at the soldier. He towered over the screaming man, and he was broader too. His blond hair was longer, shaggier when compared to the majority of what she assumed to be military regulation close-cropped cuts on the other men. He looked like a surfer, and his drawl made him sound slow and easy.

The expression on his face was anything but, and she knew instantly that this was the same man who'd scared the hell out of her in the rain. If Mrs. Mueller hadn't told her he was military, she'd have known it for sure. It was the command in his voice, the way she felt instantly protected next to him.

But the hair...

Hanny looked between Kayla and the soldier expectantly. The yelling man lowered his voice, looked suddenly humbled.

"Maybe you should apologize to Miss..."

"It's Kayla."

"Sorry," the now-cowed man mumbled and looked grateful when she nodded.

He escaped into the crowd and the soldier/surfer named Teige turned to her with the most amazing looking green eyes—jungle-green—she decided, and asked, "You all right?"

"Yes, fine."

"You're the photographer."

"And you're the one who doesn't like his picture taken."

"Guess no further introductions are necessary. Come on, Hanny." He started to walk away, but instead of following him, Hanny lay down at her feet.

He called to the dog again. Hanny put her head down on her paws and stared up at Kayla, purposely ignoring her owner. Kayla bit her lip to keep from laughing. Teige was outwardly keeping his cool but the frustration in his eyes was unmistakable—and priceless.

Payback—and karma—were bitches indeed.

"She can stay with me," she offered sweetly.

He pressed his lips together in a grim line, like he was in the midst of battle. "I'll be back," he said tightly, like he didn't want to be there at all.

Join the damned club, she thought. Mrs. Mueller had called over to the house about ten that morning, said something about a town picnic in the park and how it was a great time for Kayla to meet people.

"You'll come with me," she'd said firmly, and Kayla knew there was no reason to argue, so she hadn't. Instead, she'd helped Mrs. Mueller carry fresh-baked pies into the crowded park. Mrs. Mueller was the type to hound her if she didn't show her face in town and make some introductions. And that was the point—she needed to let the small town get to know her. They would be her best protection, because they'd tell her if a stranger came around asking questions.

She felt guilty about dragging innocent people into her problems, but she understood that it might be her best line of defense.

It's been over six months, and that's a good sign.

But it wasn't good enough. Never would be.

She'd been sitting at the picnic table for the better part of an hour before Hanny rescued her. She'd forced herself to look around, to try to spot anyone or anything unusual. Next to her, Mrs. Mueller had chatted with some women and Kayla hadn't attempted to join in. The people she'd been introduced to gave her easy smiles, assuming she was shy and overwhelmed.

She was both, and hadn't been able to get her bearings in a very long time. This was too much, too soon. Meeting the entire town wasn't what she had on her agenda.

When she'd checked in that morning with her handler, Abby gave her the *no news, good news* speech and then told Kayla it was part of the plan to make friends, to let people know her.

"You'll stick out like a sore thumb as the hermit. Small towns protect their own. Use that," Abby said.

"I don't like using people."

"Then don't. Make some friends."

She'd almost asked, "Why bother?" but it sounded too pathetic, even to her own ears.

She'd brought her camera—her talisman—the strap hanging comfortingly around her neck. If she took photos, she could get a good sense of who belonged and more importantly, who didn't. She could ask Mrs. Mueller to help her with names and faces later, after she printed the pictures.

She picked up the camera and began to take some shots of Hanny, who, she discovered, was both a complete ham and totally photogenic. Then she moved on to snapping Mrs. Mueller and the women at the table, also hams after a slight bit of convincing. They were having a lot of fun, hugging one another while mugging for the camera.

Kayla found that most of the time, those who protested having their pictures taken only needed a little coaxing before they were posing like models. She moved the camera over the crowd, capturing the little kids in the wading pool some smart parent had brought, and also took several shots of kids flying down a Slip 'N Slide, crashing into one another on the wet grass.

They were so free. Laughing. It made Kayla smile, actually, and it felt good. Until she turned to find Teige in her viewfinder's focus.

Immediately, she dropped the camera, let it hang by the neck strap.

He looked at her defiantly. She assumed her look was similar.

He handed her a soda anyway, sat down at the edge of the picnic table bench, his back to the women. Mrs. Mueller pretended not to notice, but she did a piss-poor job of it by moving herself and the other women away.

Hanny was still glued to Kayla's side. Teige mentally called the dog a traitor and he swore she snorted at him.

"Looks like you've got yourself a new protector," he said finally, and for a second an unreadable expression flickered across her face. And Teige was the master of reading expressions.

She pet Hanny, running her fingers through her thick fur. Right hand, no ring. No tan line.

Good.

"You came here with Willa?"

She nodded. "She wants to read my tarot cards."

"She refuses to read mine."

"Why's that?"

"An old superstition her husband had. Far as I know, she's never read any military man or woman's cards."

"People take her seriously?"

"Some people do." He glanced at her as he opened his soda. "And I guess you're not one of them."

"I'm not crazy about anyone knowing my future. Maybe not even me."

"I hear you."

"She said you wouldn't be home a lot."

"She's right." He paused, then held his hand out. "I'm Teige."

She accepted the gesture. Her palm was cool, soft. He wanted to rub it against his face.

He was losing his fucking mind and it wasn't going to be pleasant.

"Mrs. Mueller calls you a very nice man."

"And what have you been calling me?"

"An asshole," she said and he almost shot the soda through his nose. Recovered. Realized he was in big damned trouble here.

"Thanks for grabbing Hanny," was all he said before whistling to the dog. This time, Hanny actually followed him and neither of them turned to look back at Kayla, who was definitely watching them leave.

Chapter 6

HANNY STOOD guard while he attempted to sleep but even she was restless. Out of sorts.

Like dog, like master.

He finally surrendered to the inevitable, jacked himself up with caffeine, went through his email and voice mail, ready to field the next job offer.

A couple had him leaving tomorrow. Too soon.

Two years ago he would've jumped at them.

The one for two weeks out looked promising. High danger equaled higher pay. He answered the email and closed the laptop. He spent the rest of the afternoon on the couch, watching old movies. Just before night fell, he stretched and went out to the back porch. Last night's summer storm hadn't done much more than down a few branches here, but the local news confirmed twisters wreaked havoc in a town that was only fifteen miles away. He'd been involved in some aftermath cleanup when he was enlisted. Fucking heartbreaking to go through the shards of someone's life, finding the occasional teddy bear mixed in with the debris. He could only imagine what was happening over there today and he switched off the news, unable to bring himself to watch it.

At least he was starting to learn his limits

He glanced over at the blue house when he heard Kayla calling goodnight to Willa, and wondered if she was going to tell Mrs. Mueller about what happened last night. From the warm greeting Willa had given him at the picnic, it appeared Kayla hadn't as of yet. He walked back through his house with Hanny at his heels to stare out his side window.

Her truck had been parked all the way up the driveway. A big truck with tinted windows. Not the type a single woman typically drove. Georgia plates.

It was also a big house for a single woman. Granted, the price tag wasn't astronomical out here in the semi sticks, but still...

Not your problem.

"Don't even think about it," he told Hanny, who was paws-up on the windowsill next to him, watching Kayla as well.

She was skittish. Angry too, although he'd watched her bite it back. She acted like a woman in trouble, at least to his practiced eye. With the law? He made a mental note to find out her full name and run it to see if anything came up.

Damn, he was a suspicious bastard. He hated it, but he was wired this way and fighting it hadn't ever done him any good. And someone whose name showed nothing in the system always signaled trouble.

She's not your problem.

His attention was pulled from Kayla to a splash of red.

Diane. And she *was* his problem. She parked her flashy car in his driveway and gave Kayla a hard stare. He wouldn't be surprised if Diane pissed in a circle around his lawn. She'd always been possessive. The problem was, she'd never been in love with him. He wasn't in love with her either, so in that regard, they'd been well matched. They were good together in bed, but they brought out the absolute worst in each other in all other regards.

He waited for her to ring the bell, prepared to ignore her. But she let herself in with the key he'd given her years ago, the one she swore she'd lost.

He held out his hand and she tossed it to him.

"I thought we broke up," he said.

She watched his face for a long moment, like she was reading him. Good fucking luck.

"I thought you might need some help with a welcome home." She began to undress in his front hallway, her tank top tossed carelessly aside to reveal high, rounded breasts, her jeans already unbuttoned to show a hint of her smooth belly and no doubt, no underwear at all. "Well?"

"I'm thinking."

"You think too much."

"That's not one of your problems."

"You're a funny man." She skimmed her jeans off and threw them at him, his jab not bothering her. Nothing did, except when Teige tried to end things and then she'd buck.

He caught the soft denim and folded them, hung them over the bannister.

"I'll never be able to find another man who does the things you do to me," she'd always tell him, usually post-sex.

And Teige did have a need for control in the bedroom for as long as he could remember. Finding women to go along with those kinks had never been a problem. Hell, it seemed to push women in his direction, although the need to do so was deep-seated, born and bred, not something he trotted out to attract them.

Diane made sure to spread the word about what he liked. She also slept with other men in order to make him jealous.

Didn't work.

"I'm using you," he told her flat-out.

"Same here," she told him coolly. Hanny growled her disapproval at both of them and slunk away.

He threw her over his shoulder roughly and then bound her to his headboard with leather straps and delayed her orgasm to the point of madness, thinking about Kayla all the while. About pulling Kayla out into the rain and taking her on the soft, wet ground.

He came twice before he untied Diane and told her to take care of herself. She did, because that was what she liked—the orders. But she didn't want anything beyond the sex and he felt like an empty wrapper.

And when it was over and they both stopped panting, he said, "You can leave now."

"You bastard."

"I never promised otherwise."

"Who else are you going to find?"

"I didn't say I was going to find anyone."

"You're looking at Ms. Vanilla next door? You think she's going to let you tie her up and fuck her—"

"Shut up and leave."

"You're a freak. Everyone knows it," Diane taunted, knowing she could easily goad him. Sometimes, if he was feeling particularly dark, more sex would follow and he knew that's what she was looking for.

He didn't take the bait and that made her rant at him all the way to the bathroom, where he heard her breaking things.

He'd spent time as a young boy wondering if he was exactly that, a freak. It was only after getting the guts up to explore it further that he accepted he was born wanting sex this goddamned way. Needed it in all its hard, hot, dominating glory.

The past several years, he'd had the wrong partner, had taken things too far. Diane liked pain far more than he liked to give it. And after Mac's death, he went to a dark place, didn't think he was worthy of different.

Diane loved that.

But when he saw Kayla, he wanted different so badly. She had enough of an edge, and no matter what Diane said, Kayla could handle him.

And she wanted to. He knew that for a fact.

He heard Hanny bark, coupled with the familiar sound of her heavy paws slamming against the screen door. Except this time, there was a snap that spoke of her escape, and he knew exactly where his dog was heading as he yanked on jeans.

"Where you going, darling?"

He barely glanced at her. "You need to be out of here by the time I get back. This is it, Diane. I mean it."

"You always do, honey," she called to him as he slammed the back door behind him.

Teige hadn't seemed upset when Kayla had called him an asshole, but then again, it wasn't exactly a compliment.

Teige. She liked the name. He was handsome, but still dangerous. And she had no time for any of that in her life.

Teige also had a girlfriend. A jealous one, if the daggers she'd shot at Kayla were any indication.

Honey, you have no idea how little that scares me, she'd wanted to tell the tall blond, but she'd pressed her lips together instead before going inside. She was losing precious sleep time and she couldn't afford to fall asleep again tonight. She'd print the photos to keep her busy through the night and she'd start memorizing the faces.

Tomorrow, she'd make an album with Mrs. Mueller. Maybe she'd even go to the diner. Try to grow some roots.

Erasing yourself was a lot like committing suicide, she'd decided a long time ago. Taking yourself off the grid, disconnecting from everyone and everything you knew, was harder than it sounded. It left her alone and paranoid, too scared to get close to anyone.

Then again, there was good reason for that.

She'd deleted her hard drive before this latest move, cleaning the camera's memory card as well, deleting all pictures of any of the places she'd tried to root in, and the ones she hadn't for good measure. She thought of the plants her mom used to cultivate, how she'd start them off in a kitchen glass until the brown roots began to spider out, floating with a slimy film in the clear water.

Roots, yes, but they weren't rooted until they were in the ground. Kayla knew how they felt.

She locked the doors, checked the cameras and alarms and then texted Marshal Daniels—the twice-a-day *I'm home and alive* one they'd decided on for the next month until Kayla got settled.

She took Teige's picture out of the drawer, knew she should rip it up, and not only because he'd told her to. But she couldn't, not yet, and so she put it back under the phone book, shut the drawer and went to take a long, cool shower.

She padded downstairs an hour later in black leggings and an old broken-in T-shirt and was grateful Mrs. Mueller had pushed the to-go plate on her. She ate a sandwich as she glanced at the TV, then settled in on the couch, thinking she could sleep here with the sunlight blazing in through the windows. That if she closed the back door, locked up, she could doze off safely.

She heard the footsteps creaking upstairs, automatically looked to the security camera and saw nothing. She went back upstairs, gun in hand, just to be sure.

The rocking chair in the small room was rocking, as if someone had just gotten up from it. She felt the chill and then it passed. "Nice to see you too," she murmured, went back downstairs and made a mental note to mention this to Mrs. Mueller. Maybe she could get a reduction in rent with a roommate.

Before she could sleep, she decided to finish up a few things. Tied up the garbage neatly, because she wouldn't be going to put it out in the dark. She opened the door, and seconds later a giant dog hurtled through the old screen, ripping it neatly in half.

"Are you trying to give me a heart attack?" she asked the wiggling, barking Hanny. "And did you hurt yourself?"

She inspected the dog, saw a scrape on her nose where the screen had snagged her. "Let me fix that up."

"Shit." Teige was standing in the wreckage of the door. "She never does this."

In response, Hanny sat quietly and looked between them.

"The door was old." She pushed a hand through her still-damp hair, realized she'd forgotten her glasses upstairs. And her bra. The T-shirt was thin—see-through on the best of days. She was so not company-ready.

"Teige, honey, I'm going to make us some dinner," the blond was calling from his back porch, and when Kayla glanced out she saw the women was dressed in nothing more than the T-shirt Teige had on in the park. He was bare chested, and he didn't flush when she looked between him and the blond. But she did, her face hot.

Since the blond chick was wearing Teige's tee, that easily made her the winner.

"Hanny can stay here," she blurted out, because she didn't know what else to say.

"Doesn't look like she'd have it any other way. I'll pick her up later."

"That's fine. I don't sleep much."

"I know."

Chapter 7

TEIGE HAD COME by for Hanny sometime after eleven. She noted that the red car left his driveway long before, and that he was dressed to go running, just as he'd been the other night.

She guessed there hadn't been any dinner with the blond, and that made her stupidly happy.

Hanny perked up when she saw the leash and Kayla did the same upon seeing Teige and told herself to stop it. Teige looked like his mind was somewhere else—he didn't say much except "Thanks," before he led Hanny outside. Man and dog took off in a happy rush into the woods.

She stayed up all night, printing out the pictures, realizing she hadn't paid any attention when Mrs. Mueller was introducing people. They all looked nice. Regular people, going about their day.

She was the new girl.

By nine the next morning, she was starving. She locked the house up, left the cameras on, the portable hookup in her bag with the camera. After she ate, she might go down to the lake Marshal Daniels mentioned, to take some pictures. Inside the safety of the car, with its tinted windows, she felt foolish at how nervous she was.

"You're being ridiculous," she told herself, and decided that maybe there was something to being a hermit after all. In this day and age, you could have just about everything delivered directly to you. She never had to worry about coming into contact with people.

Isolating yourself is the worst thing you can do, Marshal Daniels would lecture her.

"I know, I know," she muttered as she backed out of the driveway, studiously ignoring anything to do with Teige's house.

Today she'd worn old, comfortable jeans, a black sweater over her tank top. Black Keds.

"You look like a woman who needs a good night's sleep," she muttered to herself, flipping up the mirror without bothering to adjust anything. Nothing was going to change.

The lot was crowded, the diner more so. She walked in and the old-fashioned bell attached to the door rang, signaling her arrival. Everyone, it seemed, turned to look at her and she gave a brief smile and headed to the closest empty table—thank God there was one—and pretended to study the menu as if her life depended on it.

This was a huge mistake.

"Kind of like being the new kid on the first day of school." The tall redhead with the wide smile slid into the seat across from Kayla. She'd brought her glass of soda with her, and she looked familiar. Kayla mentally scrolled through the pictures and recalled her as part of the crowd at Mrs. Mueller's table at the picnic.

"Hey, I'm Penny. We met yesterday but I'm sure you were pretty overwhelmed. Heard you moved into the old Kennen place."

"Mrs. Mueller didn't tell me the house had a name." She flashed to the odd noises. "Don't tell me Kennen died in the house?"

Penny laughed. "Yeah. But don't worry—Old Man Kennen was cool. A retired general. Rumor is, he still haunts around the place, keeping things in order."

"I might've heard him," Kayla admitted and Penny's eyes grew wide.

"Man, I so have to sleep over and hear it for myself. We'll do a movie night. I'll cook and everything."

"Good, because I don't."

This was nice. Easy. The way it was supposed to be. Eventually, Penny would ask more questions, but for now she seemed content with this.

As she and Penny continued their easy repartee, Kayla sat back in the chair and actually felt herself relax a little. She glanced around, feeling a little less on display. This was obviously the hot spot. She recognized a few more people from the picnic in the sea of faces, but here, families were more orderly, apparent as babies sat in mother's laps and boys sat next to their fathers, eating pancakes and eggs.

She'd never been a big breakfast fan. She ordered a chocolate shake and a BLT instead and the waitress didn't blink an eye.

"My boyfriend's in the Army—he's a Ranger. We live together three blocks over." Penny pointed toward a booth where Kayla saw the back of a man's head.

"That must be hard—all the separation."

Penny shrugged. "I'm an Army brat, so I guess I'm used to it. We moved constantly when I was younger—every two to three years we were stationed in a different country. I can curse in nine languages."

"That probably comes in handy."

"You have no idea." Penny sipped her soda and pointed at the camera. "Plans for the day?"

"I was thinking about going to the lake."

"It's pretty there." Penny sat back. "Do you take posed pictures of people?"

"Um, sure."

"I could use some new headshots."

"For modeling?"

Penny burst out laughing. "Thanks for the vote of confidence but no, I'm a character actor. I've done a few commercials—very small stuff. The pictures would be for my look book, when I go on auditions. I'd need different looks, to show I can play different roles. I'd give you full credit."

Even though it would be under her new, false name, Kayla's gut twisted at the prospect.

It must've shown through on her face because Penny simply said, "You let me know when you have time. No pressure. We just like to help out our locals." Penny looked up and waved at whoever came in and Kayla made a note to never sit with her back to the door again. "Your buddy with the dog."

"He's my neighbor," she offered and Teige walked by with a slight nod in their direction. She automatically looked back to see if Hanny—or the girlfriend—was behind him, but he was alone.

"What did Willa tell you about him?" Penny asked.

"Not much."

"Oh."

"Well, you can't stop now," she said and Penny grinned and lowered her voice as she confided, "He's been written about in some books—and portrayed in movies for his part in some famous missions. It's one of those things people around here know, but no one asks him about."

"But he's out of the military, right?"

Penny shrugged. "Men like him don't ever talk about their military jobs. And just because he's out doesn't mean he's not doing similar work, like those private contractors in Fallujah. You know, like mercenaries."

"Teige is a mercenary?" That certainly fit—she'd sensed he was a dangerous man, but even though he frustrated her, she wasn't scared of him.

"Rumor has it."

"His dog likes me. Him, not so much."

"Don't you remember elementary school? It's always the reverse of how they act." Penny looked like she wanted to say more but didn't.

The waitress put down Kayla's food and shake with an approving nod as she left.

"They don't like new people who come in and order egg white omelets and other diet food. Here, they like to feed you until you drop," Penny explained just as Teige came back their way and sat at their table without a word. The waitress brought his meal a minute later. Penny raised her brows, wrote her number on a napkin and slid it across the table. "Call me anytime about the photos."

After she left, Teige picked up a fry. "More pictures?"

"Some people actually like having their picture taken," Kayla said as casually as she could.

"Are you one of them?"

"No." She paused. "Are you the welcoming committee?"

"Do I look like the person the town would entrust that job to?" He pushed the plate of fries between them.

"Is this a peace offering?"

"They're fries."

"Who has fries for breakfast?"

"Anyone who runs fifteen miles a day," he offered, and she didn't run at all, because she was too thin anyway. He pointed to her BLT and her shake with raised brows in a *pot meet kettle* sort of way.

He didn't apologize for the incident with the camera, still wasn't going to. A peace offering was the best she could hope for and it wasn't bad at all. She gave a small grin and had a few fries. They went perfectly with the chocolate shake. Reminded her of some of the more pleasant memories of childhood, when her parents did everything they could to give her a normal life.

He looked at the pile of photos she'd set down.

"From the picnic. You can look," she offered. *None of you.*

He took them, gave her a wry smile like he'd heard that last part. His big hands dwarfed the pictures as he sifted through them. "These are good."

"Thanks."

"Do you know any of the people you took the pictures of?"

"I know Mrs. Mueller."

"Taking pictures to learn names is a good trick," he said, and although that wasn't exactly the entire reasoning behind it, she nodded and allowed him to write out the names for her in light pencil, borrowed from the waitress, along the backs of the photos. "I'll let Willa fill you in on the details surrounding them. I don't want to take away her fun."

"Ha." She took a drink from her shake. "She does make a good welcome wagon."

"I thought that was my job."

"I wouldn't count on it being a permanent position."

He smiled when she said that, then concentrated on the new plate of fries the waitress placed down beside him.

"Sundays he eats three or four plates while he's reading the paper," she told Kayla.

"Maybe you should just bring them on a bigger plate," he groused to the waitress who wagged a finger at him and then winked.

When she left, Kayla told him, "I didn't mean to invade your privacy."

"Then why did you?" He was referring back to the pictures she'd taken that first night, and his tone was part defiance, mixed with curiosity.

"Because you looked beautiful. I wanted to be a part of it."

His expression told her he hadn't expected her answer. She hadn't expected to blurt that out and she fought the urge to get up, leave—or at the very least, go hide in the bathroom.

But she didn't. Speaking what was on her mind was something no one could take from her, not in situations like this. "Mrs. Mueller said that you were away a lot. And since Hanny seems to like me, I wouldn't mind taking care of her when you're gone."

"Good protection, right?"

He'd seen the security cameras, no doubt about it. "Yes. Good company too."

"I never know exactly how long I'll be gone. Might be a week. Maybe longer."

"That's okay. I'm freelance. I'm around all the time."

He nodded curtly. "I'm not leaving for at least a week. When I do, I'll give you my friend's number, so if Hanny gets to be too much for you—"

"She won't."

He gave a small smile and ate some more fries. He was about to say something else but that tall blond strolled in and she swore Teige's entire demeanor changed. His shoulders tensed, his expression hardened and she mirrored his mood as the woman the waitress called Diane waved to a few people in the diner.

Of course she'd seen Teige, but she focused her gaze on Kayla, her eyes boring into her.

"I've got to go, okay? Just let me know when you're

dropping Hanny off. You know where I live." She tried to sound upbeat but failed. Teige nodded and she was all but forgotten again.

Beautiful. In his entire goddamned life no one had called him that, at least not to his face. The thing was, she meant it. And it warmed him in a way he thought he couldn't be.

"Teige."

Diane. Wrong time, wrong place, as always. "I told you last night that we're done and I meant it."

She gave a small pout that might've worked on him once, years ago. When he'd walked back into the house last night, he'd known that her idea of dinner meant more sex. And that's when he'd told her to leave.

Now she said, "I'm not staying away from the diner."

"You don't get it, Diane."

"Does your new plaything?"

"Stay away from her," he warned, not looking back in Kayla's direction.

Diane crossed her arms across her breasts, leaned over and whispered, "Or what? You'll spank me?"

What the hell had he ever seen in her? He blamed the jungle, got up from the table and brushed past her without another glance in her direction.

Kayla didn't want to walk by Diane, who was still talking to someone at the door. Instead, she went toward the back and stopped at Penny's table. Penny's boyfriend was in green camouflage pants and a khaki colored T-shirt, his tags tucked inside.

"I'm sorry to interrupt, but I'll do those pictures if you want."

"Oh cool! John, this is Kayla—she's the new girl," Penny bubbled as John shook Kayla's hand. "When can we do them?"

"Anytime you want."

"I have time this afternoon—the lake background would be awesome and the weather's perfect, don't you think?"

Kayla nodded. Penny seemed nice enough and Kayla wanted to help. She knew headshots were notoriously—and ridiculously—expensive, and she could give Penny some great ones at half the price.

"What should I wear?"

"They always tell you to stay away from black, but I can work with any color. Put your makeup on heavier than normal or you'll look washed-out."

"Got it. What time?"

She checked her watch. It was already half past ten. "How about an hour? Will that give you enough time?"

"Plenty, yes. John needs to go save the world anyway."

John laughed a little and Kayla noted how easy things were between them. "I'm going to the lake now to do some test shots."

"Give me your phone number, just in case," Penny said, and Kayla recited the new numbers she'd memorized.

"I texted you so you'll have mine. And thanks, Kayla. You're totally saving my life."

Kayla just nodded, her belly tightening, and walked out. Teige was gone, but Diane was still there, staring her down. Kayla smiled, because she had a feeling she'd won this round.

Chapter 8

SHE WAS at the lake for an hour before Penny came. She'd taken a few pictures but mostly she lay on the grass and stared up at the sky, enjoying the quiet. She didn't dare close her eyes, because she knew when she woke up she'd be disoriented and she hated that.

She heard Penny call her name and then she was next to Kayla on the grass. She'd brought a bag of clothes, wore a simple white collared shirt and more makeup than she had that morning.

"You look great," she told Penny, who blushed a little.

"Thanks. I went to cosmetology school. I figured it would come in handy. Oh, and listen, I forgot to ask how you wanted to be paid. I'm assuming cash?"

"Cash would be fine. And you can credit the shots in your portfolio to KC Photos, okay?"

"Fine with me. Do you have a website?"

"No."

Penny assumed there was an ex Kayla was hiding from, and whether it was a husband or boyfriend, it didn't matter. The town had its share of secrets and Kayla seemed nice. Friendly-ish. And she was doing Penny a heck of a favor.

Kayla picked up the camera and motioned where Penny should stand. Penny took direction well, and she also had fun with the shoot.

"Put your chin down," Kayla directed. "Smile smaller."

"You're a real pain in the ass," Penny teased without moving her lips.

"Tell me something I don't know." Kayla's perfectionistic tendencies were shining through full force. It was the only way she knew how to do this.

Penny wasn't conventionally beautiful, but she had an interesting face. The camera really liked her; the angles were perfect. She would get work from them, and in between smiles and serious poses, Penny explained that she'd be happy doing commercials and B-type movies. She wasn't expecting much but she had a goal.

After two hours and a couple of quick changes behind a towel, Kayla had what she needed. She showed Penny several of them on the viewfinder while she held her breath.

"These are great—oh my God, Kayla!" Penny threw her arms around her. "You've made me look so good."

"You're really pretty, Penny. It wasn't hard to do."

Penny waved her off and then continued to stare at herself in the viewfinder. "How soon can we get these into my book and onto my website?"

"I'll email them to you when I get home. I'll touch up anything that needs to be touched up, like this smudge of makeup here. I'll crop some of the background too and then they're all yours."

"Great." Penny stuffed her things into her bag. "Are you coming?"

"I'm going to stay here for a bit longer."

"Please, come over to Mo's Bar later. I'll buy you a drink."

"Maybe."

"Come on, Kayla. Single girl, fun bar, good music—and I know a million guys in this town who'd want to date you."

Kayla smiled a little at that. "I'll think about it."

"Be there at ten. I'll call and bother you if you're not. Oh and here's one of the books I was talking about where Teige's mentioned," she explained as she handed Kayla a paperback she'd pulled from her bag. "Could give you some insight."

"He's got a girlfriend."

"Ex. They're not exactly the best couple. Diane's an asshole." Penny shrugged. "She sleeps with everyone."

Kayla couldn't imagine Teige dealing well with that, so maybe he really didn't care. "Thanks. I'll return it when I'm done."

"The thing about Teige is...he's tough. Women flirt with him but most stay away because of Diane. She tends to get in people's faces," Penny told her, and then called over her shoulder as she left, "I think he likes you."

Kayla thought it was more like making amends with

the neighbor, but she wasn't about to add to the gossip. If Penny noticed, so did the rest of the town.

She'd had her business spilled to the general public more than she cared to remember. To finally have some privacy, to rely on it for survival, was novel. Now she had to crack the door a little and she thought she might be okay with it. But the more Penny talked, the more Kayla realized she hated it.

Penny had done nothing wrong. She was simply living. Sharing. She was happy and it showed...and it shoved, then stabbed Kayla in the heart as sure as a knife.

Because Kayla was attempting to immerse herself in all of that, and it was all fake, at least on her end.

These people bonded. Had real lives. She had nothing; never had, never would.

She thought about that as she snapped the afternoon sunlight dappling the water, and continued ruminating as she left the park. As she drove, she noted all the people coming and going, moving along with their lives, and it made her irrationally furious. She barely made it home, her hands shaking on the wheel. When she got inside, the anger had built to such proportions it actually scared her. She trembled as she shut the alarm and re-armed it, barely made it to the bathroom before she threw up, heaving her guts out over the toilet.

She remained on her knees on the cold, hard tile for a long while before sinking down to rest her cheek on the floor.

"This isn't working." But nothing had to this point and if she were honest with herself, nothing ever would.

She dragged herself out of the bathroom without brushing her teeth. The sour taste propelled her forward as she dialed the marshal's number.

Abby answered on the first ring. Obviously, she had no life either, but by choice. Kayla almost started with that but instead choked out, "I can't fucking do this."

"Do what?"

"Play normal. Nothing is. This is such bullshit and you know it." She hated the desperate, clawing sound of her voice, hated that she had to beg like this. When she knew nothing would or could change for her. That all she'd hear were soothing words and platitudes telling her to be strong.

Bullshit, all of it.

"Your life sucks, but you're alive," Abby told her finally. "That's my goal—to keep you alive. What's yours?"

Taken aback, she blinked. Wiped her mouth on the back of her hand. The viciousness inside returned. "Fuck you, Abby. I'm not allowed to have goals without the permission of the marshals."

"You don't have to stay under protection—it's your choice."

"Right."

"Right," Abby echoed. "You could help yourself, Kayla. You told Hoss you could feel Mara, but you never do shit about it. You've never told the police or the profilers that."

"I don't know where she is—it's not like I have GPS tracking for those feelings."

"It's a hell of a lot more than they have," Abby pointed out. "That's why they're all suspicious of you, so suck it up. You can have as empty or as full of a life as you want.

What exactly did you give up when you entered WITSEC? Hanging around, screwing, drinking, drugging? Whining about how you don't know what you want to be when you grow up? Yeah, I really feel bad for you that you had to give up all of that. I really do."

Abby's tone was dry, all sarcasm, zero sympathy. In all her years in WITSEC—hell, in all her years, no one had ever spoken to Kayla like that.

"Fuck you," she told Abby before she hung up on her, because she had no idea what to say in response.

Never let it be said she didn't run from the truth.

The anger was of course, worse. She'd never had a picture-perfect life, and that wasn't her fault. None of it was.

Victim of extreme circumstances. That phrase had been bandied around the trial, but never about her. No, Kayla had become that without anyone bothering to bestow the title.

She printed out the first of Penny's pictures and then she viciously stabbed at it with a pen to destroy Penny's smiling face, then ripped it in half and slammed the old rolltop desk closed before biting back what would turn out to be gut-wrenching sobs.

She missed Hoss. He'd been the one to give her the camera. When she was eighteen and sitting in hotel rooms at night with nothing to do but ruminate, Hoss began to sneak her out. Some of her first pictures were of the beach at night. Coney Island. She'd learned the impact of shadow versus light quickly, an apt metaphor for her life.

She credited Hoss with a lot. She'd repaid him by putting his life in danger. He'd signed up for that life, but she bet none of them thought they'd be the ones to die for the job.

She'd found his body. More blood on her hands. Why Mara hadn't used that opportunity to take Kayla didn't surprise her. Mara had plans to hurt more people, and she was prepared to make Kayla suffer along the way.

Mara wanted her sister as alone and isolated as she was.

Claire knows why I did it. Always has. She puts on a good act, pretends to be innocent. But she's the one who started it all. She was braver than me. She showed me the way and then she abandoned me. Turned against me. I didn't lose faith, not until the trial. And then I knew she'd have to pay for not believing.

The notes from Mara started coming to her, mixed in with the hate mail Kayla still received, the day after Hoss's funeral. Abby missed the service, because she was gathering up the newly renamed Kayla, trying to hold her together so she could disappear again.

Abby could've said no to the case, and maybe should've, but when she'd opened her mouth to refuse, an "I'll be on the next flight," came out instead. Just like that, she'd relocated to North Carolina with Kayla. And Abby didn't try to bullshit herself—this was all personal. She just couldn't figure out why.

You'll get what's coming to you, Abigail, just like your father did.

Plenty of people spoke those same words every single day—no one had a monopoly on them. But in that night's haze of terror, those were the only words she remembered clearly.

Was this what was coming for her? She switched on the DVD—converted recently from VHS since this was an active case—and deliberately muted it, watching Mara on the stand during her trial.

The young woman was quiet and reserved. There was no anger, no defensiveness. Her eyes were wide, shone with innocence and the familiar quiver of fear rode up Abby's spine.

She stared between the young woman giving testimony and the picture of Kayla on the desk in front of her, trying to reconcile the two.

There was no recent picture of Mara. Thanks to Kayla, it wasn't necessary.

Being the identical twin of a killer had to be the bane of Kayla's existence. Especially when she hadn't been believed—not fully. The jury convicted Mara of murdering one of the girls she'd called a friend, but they'd never fully believed she'd worked alone.

Mara had planted a seed of doubt that she'd murdered at Kayla's bidding, and even though there wasn't a shred of evidence against Kayla—and she'd never stood trial for the crime—Kayla had never been able to shake off the accusation. The scrutiny Kayla endured was incredible. Not that she'd been a saint about it. Kayla had bite, to use one of her mentor's favorite expressions. On the stand, Kayla had come across as the tough one, with Mara seeming the weaker of the two. That made it hard for the jury to reconcile the killings, and the prosecutor had done a tremendous job shifting the blame to Kayla.

Going into hiding had saved her from being the target of death threats from Sadie Jane's family. Mara had been sentenced to spend time in a psychiatric facility. Her lawyer had made a very convincing argument that after all Mara had been through in her life, she'd had a psychotic break.

The jury had vacillated between complete horror and sympathy. Kayla's angry testimony had been the nail in the coffin.

Mara had escaped from the hospital the same evening she'd been processed.

Hoss hadn't been convinced of Kayla's innocence either, but that hadn't stopped the marshal from risking—and ultimately losing—his life for her.

"How did Mara find you, Hoss?" Abby muttered for what had to have been the millionth time. She'd gone over the crime scene endlessly, questioned Kayla, who'd dealt less than patiently with the process.

Kayla had been out in the small darkroom Hoss had created for her in the unattached garage. She hadn't felt anything odd during those particular hours she spend calmly developing photos, but the day before she'd told Hoss she'd felt Mara. In the past, that always meant Mara was ready to kill.

After Mara's escape, the first thing the police had done was put Kayla in an interrogation room, and they'd kept her wrists handcuffed in front of her. She'd already been fingerprinted and the black ink was smudged on her palms because she'd fisted her hands hard. Abby watched the video of that night over and over, looking for clues.

"You have no idea where your twin is? Did you help her escape? Did you have anything to do with the murders?" the officer asked Kayla.

"Fuck you," Kayla spat back.

Her anger rang authentic to Abby. Kayla could obviously see something in her twin very few people could. Abby had also seen Kayla break down. She wasn't stone cold, and that's what gave Abby doubts about her ability to order Mara to kill Sadie Jane—or anyone.

But there was really only one way that Abby could see Mara finding where Kayla and Hoss were staying, and that was if Kayla told her. And Kayla would never do that—not purposely. And since she was very well hidden, the odds of Mara finding her were very slim. Abby had heard of twins being able to communicate, of feeling each other's pain even when they were thousands of miles apart. But for Mara to have tracked Kayla down that way seemed farfetched at best. If it was that easy, Kayla would've been able to find her sister years ago.

But Hoss was in the ground and Mara had taken credit for the kill.

I did it for you, Claire. Because you couldn't.

Kayla had been right there, close enough for Mara to kill—or at least kidnap. But she did neither of those things. It made zero sense. And it would haunt Abby until she figured out why.

Chapter 9

SHE MUST LEAVE the lights on all day. It was the only explanation as to how every light in the house was glowing brightly through the windows as soon as dusk hit, unless she had timers on all of them.

He was on the couch, on his side, facing the blue house through his own half-opened window. The ceiling fan buzzed lazily above him. He'd turned off the air conditioner earlier because he didn't want to feel comfortable, didn't want to get used to it.

He fucking did not want to keep thinking about Kayla either, but since he'd left her at the diner he'd had nothing else on his mind.

He rolled off the couch and headed to the kitchen, where he grabbed a bottled water from the fridge. He took a long gulp, then brushed the sweat from his forehead with the bottom of the T-shirt he wore before stripping it off completely. It was hot as hell in here, but he'd been in hell and he'd never complain about being home.

He'd believed in the Army. Being out after serving twenty years allowed him to use his skills without his hands being tied by red tape. Funny thing was, he still worked for all the same people, so official or not, it was the same team, the same goals.

He glanced out the window again at Kayla's fully lit-up house. Kayla was definitely keeping secrets, but she was in the right place for it. Small towns always had big secrets, and in this town, there wasn't any point in trying to keep anything to yourself. And for someone as secretive as he was, it was an odd choice of place to live. But it kept him honest. It also helped that he didn't have to talk about his military time, because everybody knew. It was the ultimate contradiction. Gossip was natural, and most of it regarding him was good-natured, if not grudgingly respectful. Which meant that Kayla knew more about him and his time in the service than she had a week ago.

But there were deeper secrets no one was privy to. The FBI's careful planning and cover-up, plus a new last name and social security number, ensured his past stayed buried as long as Teige wanted it to. Healed or not, old wounds shouldn't be fucked with.

Hanny yawned contentedly and then fell back to sleep. She was in the middle of the tiled kitchen floor, where nothing could bother her. He got down and stretched out next to her and, for the first time in weeks, slept for two hours straight.

Kayla had showered, but only to make herself feel better. She towel-dried her hair, put on some light makeup and shoved the fake glasses on impatiently.

She couldn't get used to them, but her eyes couldn't handle contacts, no matter how many brands she'd tried. There were so few ways to change her looks—she'd done every type of cut and color, and even if she'd been able to go back to her original shade, she wouldn't have wanted to. More than once, she'd wished she could permanently change her face. She'd even consulted a plastic surgeon about it, but had gotten nervous when he started asking a lot of questions. She'd been stupid to even do that, and she'd never told Hoss, even though for months afterward she'd worried she'd compromised her safety.

"You're never not worried," she told herself, then was interrupted by her ringing cell phone. Penny. She'd already left a message earlier and was, as promised, not letting Kayla out of this.

Kayla avoided looking into the desk where she'd shoved the ripped-up picture of Penny, and instead concentrated on the eight-by-ten prints she had ready and laid out on the kitchen table.

It was never about Penny. It wasn't fair to take her frustrations out on her, but Abby Daniels was fair game.

Still, she didn't pick up Penny's call, but texted her instead that she was on her way.

Penny hadn't asked any questions about her past, she mused as she threw on jeans and a tank top, a sheer white shirt over it, and brushed her quickly drying hair. Kayla was pretty sure she'd figured out something was wrong, but was smart enough not to bring it up.

It's been less than a week since you've been here—too short a time for anyone to find you.

Ten minutes later, she was driving the short distance to the bar. Teige's truck hadn't been in his driveway, but she'd heard Hanny barking as she'd left her house.

Soon, he'd be away, leaving Hanny behind for her. Her newest protector. She wondered if the dog typically stayed with Diane and decided against it. Diane didn't seem the type to take care of anything or anyone but herself.

When she pulled into the bar's lot, she checked her hair in the mirror as she dialed Penny.

Penny picked up on the first ring. "Where are you?"

"I just pulled into the lot."

"About time. I'll come outside to get you," Penny said and Kayla was grateful, because she didn't relish walking into the bar alone.

At the last minute, she took the glasses off and put them on the console between the seats before getting out of the truck.

"Glad you came," Penny said with a warm wave. "I didn't want to waste this makeup."

Penny hooked her arm in Kayla's, her enthusiasm infectious but not annoyingly so. Together, they entered the bar, which was warm and smoky and loud. And crowded. Everyone seemed to be having fun, and Penny led her to a table in the back. They ordered fried bar food and a pitcher of dark beer.

In between saying hi to people who stopped by their

table—most of whom Kayla recognized from the picnic photos—Penny talked about her boyfriend.

"We've been together for four years," she said. "I knew I loved him from the second I saw him. He took a little longer to convince."

Kayla laughed, amazed she could after her meltdown that afternoon. There was still a dark, hurting place inside her but she pushed it down until it stayed there. For how long, she had no idea.

She took a long drink of beer as she looked around the crowded bar. The music blasted and she wanted to be wild and dirty again, the way she'd been in high school, sneaking out the window, down the trellis so she could drink and smoke and spend time with boys she knew were bad for her. The badder, the better.

She'd been completely self-destructive, but she'd also recognized that to try and stop that part of her personality had been impossible. When she was fifteen, sixteen, seventeen, her emotions had constantly threatened to bubble over, and taking the edge off had been the only thing to help.

She was on that edge again. Mara was close—maybe not physically, but things were coming to a head, whether Kayla wanted to admit it or not. And so now, in this bar, she was going to do exactly what she needed to.

Penny shifted in her seat, allowing Kayla to spot Teige in the farthest dark corner. He was leaning against a tall table, his stance casual as he talked to another man. She'd bet he saw her already, because nothing got by him.

And he hadn't come over to say hi.

She bristled, felt the old anger rise and knew how dangerous that was. And she didn't care. She could try to control things as much as possible, but the reality was that she had no control over anything.

"Let's go to the bar," she told Penny now, and Penny readily agreed. They did a couple of shots each, and soon found themselves surrounded by a group of guys.

"Come on, sweetheart—dance with me," one of them urged her. He had a buzz cut, dark eyes. Friendly, open. The total opposite of Teige.

She let him take her hand and lead her to the dance floor. The first songs were fast, and then a slow ballad came on, and she waited to feel something, anything, when he held her close.

There was nothing but a dizzying drunkenness and his hot beer breath in her ear.

Maybe she should kiss him. Or maybe the other night with Teige touching her had been a fluke and she really was dead inside.

Over Buzz Cut's shoulder, she saw another guy wink at her. His hair was slightly longer and she smiled at him. Winked. Because starting trouble was the way to quell the ache inside. And when he sent over a drink, via a waitress, in the middle of the dance floor to her, she broke away from Buzz Cut to accept it.

"This is from Charlie," the waitress said and pointed. Winked at her, like, *Good going, girl, with two of them on the line.*

"Ah, sweetheart, don't let him woo you," Buzz Cut told her. "Thought you were with me."

"You'll have to try harder," she teased before lifting her glass to the longhaired guy and then downing the shot. The longhaired guy came to the dance floor just as Buzz Cut swept her into another slow dance. The anger on Buzz Cut's face was easy to read, and she didn't protest, because it felt good to push someone to that point.

There'd be trouble soon, of her own making. She wanted that energy sprawling around her. Knew this small disturbance would morph into something big and bold and careless and stupid.

That was it—she craved careless.

The longhaired man was determined to cut in. He argued with Buzz Cut and they pushed each other and she was caught between them for a few moments before rough hands—rough, wonderful hands—pulled her out of the fray that would soon consist of swinging fists and broken beer bottles.

Within what appeared to be seconds, the simple argument caught everyone up in its wake. She wanted to stay in the middle of the bar brawl, to be the center of attention, and not for the terrible, horrible reasons she'd once been.

"Let me go," she shouted, struggled against Teige's grasp. It wasn't hurting her, but it was definitely strong.

She saw Buzz Cut slam the longhaired man into the crowd before coming toward them, as if determined to keep Kayla. He was battling for her. Would Teige?

"You okay?" he called, before noting Teige's hold on her. "Get your fucking hands off her."

Teige let her go, moved forward as Buzz Cut circled him, goading him. Teige remained expressionless, but she swore he was enjoying this. The testosterone pulsed through the bar and everyone was cheering then, waiting for the fight that would ensue.

The bouncers tried to get through the crowd but couldn't. She should've been claustrophobic and if she thought about it too hard, she would be. Instead, she concentrated on Teige.

He was a blur of motion, but it was compressed—he used the least amount of movement, energy and force in order to subdue Buzz Cut.

Now, Buzz Cut's cheek was pressed into the pool table, with Teige's hand on the back of his neck. Teige whispered something into his ear and Buzz Cut nodded once.

When Teige let him up, he glared at Teige but then walked to the door and left.

In Kayla's experience, men like that didn't give up. She recalled the inherent danger in pushing men past their breaking point, because there was always a price to causing this much trouble. She looked around frantically for an alternate exit, something she normally did whenever she entered a new place. She cursed herself for being too distracted to do so this time as the familiar, hated panic set in.

You haven't changed a goddamned bit.

She tasted the bitterness of that statement on her tongue, overpowering anything else.

The panic must've shown on her face, because Teige's arm went around her firmly as he led her out the door and through the parking lot. Once at her truck, he held out his hand for her keys, an unspoken command she followed by rote.

She climbed into the passenger's seat unsteadily. He didn't help her in or close her door, took off fast as the sirens approached. She fell heavily against the seat as he careened around the corner, but before she could say anything, he said, "You started that fight."

"What do you care?"

"I don't. I like a good fight."

"Why'd you stop it, then?"

"The look on your face."

She wanted to ask him why he gave a shit, tell him he had no idea what kind of trouble she was, but she didn't. Instead, she balled her hands together on her lap. The anger radiated off her in waves as Teige steered her big truck toward home at a more normal rate of speed.

Home. How ridiculous.

"This doesn't feel like you."

He was talking about the car, his hand caressing the steering wheel. She hated that he was right. She'd have preferred something small and fast, but not a flashy red. Something black and sleek, an older model. "I like to be safe."

With that, he gave a sharp yelp of a laugh. "Bullshit."

"How would you know my stance on safety?"

"Because you called me an asshole."

"No one ever stands up to you?"

"No one smart."

"And you like it that way?"

Teige glanced at Kayla before admitting, "Most of the time."

He liked her a hell of a lot, but admitting *that* to the pretty girl with a penchant for trouble wasn't going to happen. She'd already gotten him to brawl for her, something he hadn't been goaded into since he was sixteen. "If you wanted to dance with me, you could've just asked me."

"I didn't."

"Way to bruise my ego, sweetheart," he drawled.

She blurted out, "I have this anger inside—it scares me," without looking at him.

"At least you admit it."

"What difference does that make?"

"Everyone has that inside them. It's when you pretend you don't and you act like everything's fine that gets you into trouble."

She pondered that. Maybe he was just making shit up, but she wanted to believe him.

He pulled the truck into her driveway, all the way up next to the house, the way she usually parked it. She slid out and he was by her side before she could close the door. Together, they walked up to her porch, a silent admission that he'd noticed she never used her front door, despite the fact that it was closer to where they'd parked.

She'd also noticed he had a similar aversion to his.

People were attacked more often at their front doors. Back doors gave the element of surprise. She almost said that out loud, but caught herself.

Her head was reeling and it wasn't only from the alcohol. Once on her porch, she turned and he was so damned close. She reached out and put her palms flat on his chest, noted her swollen knuckles only for a second before looking up at him.

He bent his head forward and kissed her. One of his hands wound around the back of her neck to hold her close as his mouth took hers. She fisted the front of his shirt, ignoring the jolt of pain from her injured hand as she kissed him back.

His kisses were punishing. Exciting. His kisses revealed what he wouldn't tell her. Teige would give her everything, but he'd ask for the same in return. In bed, under him, she finally wouldn't have to pretend.

He continued kissing her as her hands loosened their grip on his shirt and moved to his shoulders. He pressed her tightly to him and she felt every hard plane of his body against hers.

She couldn't get away from him physically, not unless she asked. And somehow that thrilled her in a way she couldn't explain. She had just enough leeway to rock her hips so she could rub against him, and he encouraged it, his hand moving to her ass at one point to increase the friction between them. She was wet and hot for him, and she wished she had the courage to take his hand and place it between her legs. But his mouth remained on hers, his tongue teasing and then demanding all at once. She moved her hands to his hair, twined her fingers...and his went into her hair, his grip tighter. And it turned her on even further—like she could maybe come just from this.

But just when their groping became more frantic, he

ripped away from her with a low, growling groan that shot straight to her sex.

"I don't feel like I control anything in my life," she whispered, without knowing why.

"You seem pretty in-control to me."

"Inside, I'm spinning."

"So why not make all that dizziness enjoyable." He flicked her nipple with his nail and she gasped. "Don't fight it. Kiss me again."

"You kissed me first," she murmured, but she surrendered to him because she didn't want to make any more choices. She wanted all the decisions to be his. And while she wasn't a virgin, with Teige she was definitely in virgin territory.

She'd never gotten to this point with the last guy she'd dated while in WITSEC, or any of the other men who'd taken her on dates, kissed her, attempted to touch her over these last six years.

Here, in his arms, in the dark on the creaking porch, the light from her house bathing them so Teige looked like he was glowing, she was safe. A far cry from the first night she'd met him.

There's nothing safe about this man. Not when he circled her wrists with one hand and put them behind her back so he could mouth her nipples through her thin shirt. She couldn't touch him, not when his hand dipped lower between her legs.

"Tell me what you want?" he asked.

"You. Teige. Please."

He smiled a little, that vacancy long gone from his

eyes, replaced by the most beautiful lust she'd ever seen. And then his expression faltered and he pulled back and actually stepped away from her, leaving her confused and more than a little restless. "Goodnight, Kayla. Sleep tight."

"I don't sleep at night."

"Me neither." He paused. "I leave early."

"Oh."

"I'll send Hanny over in a couple of hours."

"Okay."

"If I stayed..." He paused. "I can't stay. Not before a job. Not after a job."

She nodded, because she couldn't think of what else to say. He backed away, motioned for her to go inside while he watched, and she did, the hiss of the alarm reassuring her. The cameras showed all clear and she watched out the window as he disappeared into his own house.

She put her hand to her mouth. Her lips were swollen, hot from his kisses. Her wrists would bear slight red marks from where he'd held her fast. And she'd liked it, had rubbed against him, her body aching for more.

His walking away. Was he telling her that she couldn't handle him and all his demons? Because maybe he was right. Or maybe her demons could do battle with his and win any day.

The kiss destroyed him, brought home the reality he'd been denying for as long as he could remember, and most recently, since Kayla moved in.

The kiss—he'd given in to it, sunk against her body so easily and he'd been goddamned done for, no matter the price. He'd held her to the fit of his body—fucking perfect, like he'd known it would be.

He thought he was too hardened for this. Too alone. Too dominant for someone who seemed to have so many fears.

Then again, Kayla showed him that he had just as many fears.

Turned out the bastard Mac was right again. He'd always been goddamned right and now Teige was...

Lucky. And falling rapidly back into a past he didn't want to revisit.

Chapter 10

TWO WEEKS PASSED. Teige arrived home quietly in the middle of the night, but didn't come to get Hanny until a day and a half later. She watched him leave his house, running into the woods, not coming out for hours.

He had a bandage on his forearm. Another on the back of his neck, some bruises on his cheek.

She didn't dare take pictures of him, no matter how badly her hands itched to do so. And when he knocked on her back door after that day and a half, and she let Hanny out to greet him enthusiastically, he thanked her absently and went back into the woods after putting Hanny on a leash. Hours later, the bell rang again and Hanny walked past her into the house like she owned it, trailing her leash behind her and settling in for a long nap. Teige was walking back toward his house without so much as a backward wave.

Kayla was angry at herself for feeling wet between her

legs watching him cooling down from his run, stretching his big, scarred body.

He should terrify her. He did terrify her and still, she dreamed about having him in her bed.

During the weeks he'd been gone, she did some family portraits and took lots of shots of Hanny. Having the dog with her had made her feel more confident.

She took in his mail to her house too (and he hadn't bothered to ask for that back yet), checked around to make sure it looked okay like he'd asked. She felt a little like a voyeur and had a strange feeling Mrs. Mueller was watching. Up until now, she'd avoided the woman's attempts to read the tarot cards, but Kayla knew she was reading them with or without Kayla's consent.

She'd also read the book based on Teige's Delta Force days, and one of the most famous—and deadly—missions, and had seen a movie based on it—both had become bestsellers, although only the book had given away Teige's real name. She tried to picture Teige in those situations, running for his life in the dusty streets of countries bound with strife. Running, praying, and ultimately saving others.

It was a scripted version of him; not a bad portrayal necessarily, but now that she'd met the real thing...

Blond hair. A deep drawl. He could be mistaken for a surfer with his long, lean muscled body that at times was strung tighter than a bow.

He knew cold. Hunger. He knew fear and anger, both uncontrolled and controlled. When he came home, he no doubt despaired of things, but he walked it off and kept going.

Was there a point in time when he would be pushed beyond his limits, unable to come back from his dark place?

Wasn't she just as worried about that for herself?

The book didn't say why he'd left the Army. She was sure Penny would know, at least have a theory, but she was better off asking Teige himself about that.

"He'll be home soon," she'd promised Hanny for those weeks he'd been gone.

In reality, it had seemed like forever. She wondered how wives—girlfriends—dealt with it.

Maybe if you hadn't kissed him...

But he'd kissed her first, and it had been good. Even though she was scared of him because he'd been brutal and dangerous on his jobs—all things she'd spent her adult life avoiding—she couldn't deny she was drawn to his darkness like nothing she'd ever felt.

He might be strong enough for her. And maybe she wouldn't have to pretend anymore, wouldn't have to mute herself.

An hour after Teige returned Hanny to her, she poured Hanny some water and food for when the dog woke from napping. She was just about to look through the window again, to see if Teige was still outside chopping wood or sitting, staring into space, but before she could part the curtains, she felt the chill run through her and it wasn't the good kind of shiver. Would've screamed but that might've upset Hanny. Instead, she curled against the dog like nothing bad could happen to her if Hanny was around.

If only that were true.

She glanced at the clock—after three in the morning. She always thought that if you could get past that hour, you were okay. But nothing was.

Why Mara was quiet for so long, Kayla had no clue. Sometimes she let herself wonder what Mara did during those stretches. Did she try to have a normal life or did she spend all her time hiding, the way Kayla herself was? How did she support herself? How did she eat?

And why did Kayla care? She should hate her, but she couldn't. Mara had watched out for her for years after their adoption. Kayla couldn't forget that. It was why her testimony was ultimately so weak and unconvincing. Although it did get Mara sentenced, there was always the wash of blame on Kayla for that, like she was hiding her part in everything.

It was all her fault. And no matter how she tried to convince herself that it wasn't, that was for naught.

Finally, she was able to shake off the fear long enough to check for Teige and, true to form, he was still there, staring up at the moon. He had to feel her looking at him. She needed him so badly. To talk, to kiss. Anything. But even from a distance she could tell he was far away, too much so to comfort her. He looked like he could barely help himself and really, what would it solve? It wasn't like she could tell him what she suspected.

But she could tell Abby, even at five in the morning.

Again, the marshal answered on the first ring. She didn't give Abby a chance to say anything before telling her, "Mara killed again." She heard Abby suck in a breath and continued, "And before you ask, I don't know. Do you have any idea how shitty that feels?"

"I know."

There was such a long silence after Abby spoke that Kayla almost hung up. Instead, Kayla bit out, "Unless you had a serial killer in your family—"

"A serial killer murdered my father. In front of me," Abby said flatly. "So you don't know everything. Not by a long shot."

It was Abby who hung up this time. Kayla lay there, holding the phone, watching Teige out the window.

Everyone has their own private pain, their own secrets, Hoss used to say. You can't know someone else's suffering or judge from the outside.

She supposed that's why Abby became a marshal. Maybe Abby Daniels wasn't even her real name.

She had questions, but she wasn't about to call back and ask Abby, who probably thought she'd told too much already.

Chapter 11

ABBY TRIED to ignore the conversation with Kayla that repeated in her head over and over again.

Boundaries, Daniels. Learn them and live by them.

Like father, like daughter.

Hoss would've told her that she saw herself in Kayla, but that wasn't completely true.

Even if it was...

Ah, what the hell was she doing, beating herself up? She could do more productive things like search the database for new crimes.

Sometimes, putting the pieces together on a serial killer was a long haul. Today, law enforcement was, for the most part, savvy enough to enter crimes in a database for the FBI to draw upon. The Behavioral Analysis Unit in Quantico would contact them if there were connections to be made. Sometimes, local law enforcement would contact the BAU with questions as well.

But she also had the resources to search local crimes,

for obvious reasons. Keeping a witness safe wasn't only about placing them. It was constantly checking the environment around them for safety. Once Mara was caught, Kayla could have a more permanent placement.

She did a string search, inputting the word fire, and of course there were more hits than she cared to count, many of which turned her stomach.

She tapped the closed folder next to her on the desk again. Thought about Teige, who was just home from a job according to his most recent text. He always checked in with her like that, both when he left and when he returned, but never gave her any further information. Don't ask, don't tell was the military's motto in more ways than one. Most men's as well.

Frustrated, she paged state by state for recent crimes. Kayla had never been wrong, according to Hoss. Even the night he'd died, Kayla said she'd felt it, just had no idea how close to home it was.

She stared at the Skype icon on the iPad. It had been six-months-plus since she'd had any contact with Ethan. She'd logged in a few times recently, desperately hoping he'd see it.

Nothing.

She wanted to hate him for that, but it was what they signed on for. Ethan Graves was a CIA spook. It was like dating a ghost, but for Abby it worked. No normal boyfriend would deal well with the demands of her job or its secrecy.

Ethan had more than enough of his own secrets and she'd long ago realized that secrets didn't kill. People did.

But even for him, it had been a long time. Didn't necessarily mean something bad had happened. She'd learned that from Teige's job.

But he was away and she was alone and pissed, the same way Kayla was.

"Come on, Ethan. Please," she said through clenched teeth. But she wouldn't say she needed him. Could never bring herself to do that.

Like magic, the screen flashed under her fingers. Ethan's face came up—dark in the background, sounds of gunfire pattering through the speakers.

"You okay, Abs?"

"I'm not the one being shot at. Are you in a moving car?"

"A fast one," he agreed. "Might cut out any minute."

"What's wrong?"

"Be careful, Abs. I hate to do this shit to you, but I can't not tell you."

She knew what he was talking about. Ethan had what his mother had called "the sight." Abby hadn't believed it at first. Not until he'd made her a believer, and then he'd stopped telling her anything. Didn't want her to depend on it. Didn't want to freak her out.

Except for tonight.

Her father despised psychics. Scoffed at them, called them con men. They'd screwed up a lot of cases, hurt a lot of families.

Ethan hadn't admitted anything to her about himself until she'd known him for five years. It slipped out, bit by bit, until he'd been forced to admit it.

He hated it. Hid it from everyone.

"I'm fine," she assured him now. *I just miss you. Want you.*

He gave a wry smile, his tanned face lighting up a little, like he'd read her thoughts. The bastard. "Just watch yourself."

The screen cut out before she could tell him the same thing.

She shrugged her shirtsleeves up. Her jacket had been abandoned the minute she'd come into the office.

Her old partner retired last year. With budget cuts, she'd been working alone, expecting nothing in that regard to change. But an email did just that.

Tomorrow, she'd have a new partner. A man named Jacoby Razwell. Twenty-eight. New to the marshals' office and the rest of his background was buried, which signified he'd either had a major fuck up at his last job and knew the right people to cover his ass, or else he'd done major under-cover work with the military or an agency.

She might never know which one.

She sighed, touched the screen again like she hoped Ethan's face would pop up but it remained frustratingly blank.

Six months and finally.

Quiet for six months and now...

She leaned forward as a crime listing in Arizona caught her eye. Originally thought to be part of a brushfire. Body found. Buried.

Shit. She called the local PD and got on the phone with the chief, even before calling the FBI.

"It's US Marshal Abby Daniels. I think your Jane Doe killed in the fire has a connection to one of my witnesses. After we finish, I'll make sure the FBI contacts you. Do you have an ID?"

They did. And the name was familiar to Abby. She thanked the cop, hung up the phone and put her forehead down on the desk.

When the sick feeling passed, she typed the name in and stared at the results with unblinking eyes.

There was some kind of pattern now, and that might make things so much worse.

After waiting to hear confirmation from the FBI, which came in ten minutes later, she did the last thing in the world she wanted to do. She picked up the phone to let Kayla know she'd been right. Again.

Two more days passed before Teige came by with the same routine—grab Hanny for a middle of the night run. But this time when he returned, with Hanny in tow, he waited by her back door. He still looked vacant. All he said was, "I'm leaving again in a few days."

"I'll keep her again—no problem," she said. He nodded and she bit her tongue to stop herself from telling him not to go anywhere.

It was none of her business. Maybe it was always like this for him, for all of the soldiers.

She hadn't needed to hear from Abby to know a body would turn up, so when Abby called, she'd let it go straight to voice mail. Now, she was supposed to go to some annual block party and none of it seemed right.

Judging by the way Teige acted, she doubted he would be there.

"Does this town ever do things quietly?" she asked as she walked through the four residential streets that separated her small street from the party with Penny, and Hanny on a leash, toward the blasting music and general craziness.

"This time of year's always crazy. We see less of each other in the winter," Penny assured her with a grin. "So, what's up with you and your neighbor?"

"Oh, stop." She smiled, but inside she was all curled in the fetal position and as they got up close and personal to the party, she knew for sure she shouldn't have come. She wasn't good at making small talk to begin with.

To distract herself, she took pictures of the kids. They always posed, goofily, laughing, for her.

She wound the leash around her belt—not that it mattered, since Hanny stuck to her like glue anyway—and took a few steps back to get a shot of them hitting the piñata hanging on a nearby tree and ended up walking into Diane.

Shit. The tall, cool blond with the southern drawl was no doubt hoping Teige would be here.

Join the club, sweetheart. Kayla wished the same of the man who she'd barely seen or spoken to since he'd returned home. They certainly hadn't discussed the kiss and he hadn't seemed like he wanted to do it again.

"Sorry," she said quickly, took a few shots until Diane

walked away, but not before looking on both her and Hanny with extreme distaste. Diane's jeans fit perfectly—Kayla felt dumpy next to her. No matter how thin she got, she'd never look like that. Normally it wouldn't bother her, but the history with Teige made things so much worse. And that shouldn't matter.

You're just friends. You knew that's all there was.

Because a man like Teige would always want to only be friends with her.

The kiss was a mistake. Maybe she'd been the one to initiate it, even, and he'd just gone along with it.

"This should be interesting," Penny murmured, then clarified, "Whenever Teige and his ex are in the same place, there's always some kind of fireworks. Especially after they've broken up."

Kayla's heart jumped—she turned to see Teige talking with a group of men—and together she and Penny watched Diane approach him, and then hug him. "Doesn't look so ex to me."

"I thought you didn't care."

"I don't," she said, trying to convince herself. Hanny rubbed her head against Kayla's thigh, like she understood the headache Kayla was getting. In the past few minutes, the left side of her head began to throb, threatened to blossom into full-blown pain.

She couldn't take any precautionary meds, because the only things that truly worked tended to make her tired and goofy, and that wasn't the impression she wanted to make. She left Hanny with Penny for a moment, headed to the big cooler that held the drinks, dug for something with caffeine.

She came up with a Coke in her hand and Diane in front of her. In an effort not to appear irritated, she stuck out her hand, said, "Hi, I'm Kayla."

Diane sipped her glass of wine. "You're Teige's dog sitter, he says." Diane, with her long tapered fingers holding the elegant wine glass, and looking equally so.

Kayla forced herself not to tip the glass to spill it down her perfect white dress. "Something like that."

"That's cute. You could have a business or something, besides your little taking-pictures thing." Diane waved her free hand and Kayla had to get the hell out of here. She held the soda so hard the can crunched a little and she knew she couldn't risk opening it. Disgusted, she threw it in the trash, but Diane wasn't done. "We've been together for years, you know."

"Good for you."

Diane's smile was slippery. Fake as hell. "Teige has special...requirements in bed. Certain needs, you know? He's not a nice guy under the sheets. No one else has ever been able to handle him like I have, and he knows it."

Kayla thought about the way Teige held her wrists and her face heated as Diane smirked.

"Right—he held you down a little and it's hot at first. He starts out like that and then he gets rough." She showed Kayla near-healed bruises on her wrists. Weeks old, but they belied the violence of what had happened.

Except Diane's eyes glowed at the memory. She'd liked it. Asked for it. Kayla saw that clearly.

She continued, "There's no way you can give him what he wants. He feels sorry for you—that's the only reason he kissed you. Trust me, he comes back to me every single time. This one's no different."

"You were watching me?" she blurted out. "Don't you ever spy on me again." Her voice raised and people turned to look.

"Oh, honey, you haven't been in town long enough to know the pecking order of this place, but you are low woman on the totem pole." Diane smiled. "You don't want to mess with me."

Kayla watched her face—the smugness was what got her. "Maybe I do."

Diane lifted a brow. "What are you going to do? Give me flash burn?"

She was still laughing when Kayla clocked her across her left cheek. Diane cried out, stumbled backward then came forward to jab at her, a hand still on her jaw. Kayla pushed her back on one shoulder, not wanting this to escalate further.

"You don't want to come after me," she warned, but Diane lunged. Instinct, bred by years of street fighting like this, took over. Kayla had her by the hair, got in a punch to Diane's stomach and other cheek before they were pulled apart.

Kayla's lip bled from Diane's scratching. She had nail marks down her forearm as well. And she jerked out of Penny's grasp, walked toward the yelling woman. Lowered her voice, heard herself hiss, "You'll be sorry if you ever spy on me again."

As she pushed back past Penny, she grabbed Hanny's leash and heard Diane saying, "You heard her threaten me, didn't you?"

She kept walking, heard light footsteps behind her but didn't slow down. Penny was practically running to keep up with her, asking, "What the hell?"

"She's a bitch and a troublemaker."

"Well, yeah. And she probably deserved the punch," Penny told her, kept her voice down. "I'm sure most of the women in town will shake your hand when Diane isn't looking. But honey, you just bought yourself a mess of trouble."

"I already had it," she muttered, then stopped. "I'm heading home before I cause any more chaos at the party. You stay—make me look good."

She walked away, heard Diane yelling, "She thinks I offended her by asking about her job. It's not like she's a professional photographer or anything," to save face and Kayla decided that she hated small towns.

Dog sitter. Is that how Teige described her?

Had Teige seen the fight? Was he busy comforting Diane?

Angrily, she wiped tears from her eyes as she cut through Mrs. Mueller's backyard with Hanny at her heels. With the shepherd, she didn't feel as worried about approaching her house alone in the dark. She'd left the lights blazing, and the alarm buzzed reassuringly when she went inside. Hanny, of course, followed her, and she locked and alarmed them back in, checked the security cameras and then did her own check with her gun in hand.

The chair creaked when she walked in.

"Hello to you too. I've had a shitty evening," was all she said before leaving to go back downstairs. Took her meds, grabbed her ice pack and made some strong espresso, even though she knew it wouldn't work. Nothing ever did except crying through the pain and coming out the other end.

She sat with Hanny curled next to her on the couch, lights dimmed slightly in concession. Purposely ignored the damned phone when it started ringing.

Abby. Again. The marshal wouldn't leave a message about a body on voicemail, so all Kayla did was text, *"I don't want to know about anything right now. Migraine. Will call later,"* because she wanted to avoid a visit from Abby.

She punched her hurt fist viciously against the couch and welcomed the fresh burst of pain. She only stopped because Hanny moved closer to her, as if sensing Kayla would continue to hurt herself.

She was never more grateful for this dog's company.

Hanny got up half an hour later, tail wagging at the back door. Which meant only one thing—it was Teige, coming to collect his dog from the dog sitter for another run.

"He could at least pay me," she muttered and Hanny looked at her. "Sorry. You know what I mean."

"Kayla, open up!" he called forcefully and she shot him the finger, even though he couldn't see it. At least she didn't think he could, until it was too quiet and she glanced up to see him standing a few feet from her and her upturned middle finger.

She pulled it down slowly. He wasn't in running clothes, still dressed in the jeans he'd had on at the block party.

"I guess you know what happened," she muttered, moved aside so he could come in. Hanny already made herself comfortable in the living room. Teige set a bag of Chinese takeout down on the coffee table.

"You never use the front door," she said finally, because it was easier than talking about punching his on again-off again girlfriend.

"Don't like them," was his answer.

"Me neither."

"I don't think of you as the dog sitter."

"She's an ass but that's not why I left." It was only a partial lie. She went back to the couch and grabbed the ice packs, one for hand and one for head.

"Migraine?" he asked. She nodded and he glanced at her hand and said, "Do you need medicine?"

"I don't need you, okay? I've done this on my own for years."

He wanted to tell her that she didn't have to. At this point, he couldn't do anything but help her. Because she did need someone. And he might have read the situation wrong, but he didn't think so, not entirely. "You up for the food or you want me gone?"

"Won't Diane mind?"

"I don't give a shit about her." He looked at her. "Food? Or do you want to be alone."

"Another peace offering?"

"Honey, there's nothing peaceful about you."

She snorted, stood. But she was moving slowly. Teige lowered the lights even further and grabbed some plates from the kitchen.

Her whole house was wired, all three floors, plus the outside. Not a bad job, especially considering he didn't think she'd had any help doing it.

There was something going on here, and he forced himself not to think about it. Refused to, actually. He'd come here because he knew he had to apologize for Diane.

He thought he could handle the party, but he definitely wasn't ready to be here, with Kayla, feeling the way he did about her. Needed at least another couple of days.

You always were drawn to the danger.

She'd followed him into the kitchen, was leaning with a hip against the counter, an insolent look on her face.

To tell the truth, when he'd heard the commotion and learned she'd punched Diane, he'd almost cheered. He knew the woman had deserved it. And Kayla was the first person in this town to stand up to her.

She was defending herself...defending him. Bringing the takeout was a peace offering, a way in, but at that moment, he didn't give a shit about the goddamned food.

Chapter 12

SHE WATCHED Teige's mood change before her eyes, from one of concern to one of interrogation. She held her arms around herself, like that could brace her for the questions.

He studied her for a long moment. She took the time to do the same to him. He was still a bit off, but rapidly getting his game back, if the Teige she'd first officially met at the picnic, and later at the diner, was any indication of the way he was post-work. Although he always seemed somewhat growly, she saw the immediate difference from the man who'd insisted she delete his photos, and the one who showed up at her door two days post-mission, barely speaking to anyone but Hanny.

Now, the vacant look was gone from his eyes, just in time for the meds to begin to take effect. They always loosened her too much, made her feel more than a little sensual. Turned on. Wrong time, wrong place, wrong man.

Right time. Right place. Right man.

As she'd suspected, he didn't take the food out of the bag. Asked instead, "Want to tell me what happened?"

"Not particularly."

"Not saying she didn't deserve it. Just figure that, since it pissed you off so bad, a part of you has to feel like that's how you think I treat you."

"Soldier, psychologist," she mused with a deep sarcasm to balance out the throbbing pain in her knuckles. "And no, I'm not apologizing, if that was going to be your next question."

"It wasn't."

She put the ice on her hand and let it sit there, the sting of the cold giving its own version of pain that would soon turn numb.

"You're quick to fight."

"I've been told I have a God-given talent for it." *White trash. Trailer trash.* Those words were bandied around long after she'd left the double-wide she'd lived in until she was eight and moved in with the new family. She'd forgotten everything but how to fight and in the beginning, she had— a lot. She'd simmered down some by tenth grade, made friends with a wild crowd who liked her just the way she was.

Idiots. As she'd been.

As she obviously still was.

She'd asked Mara if the white trash label was true and, if so, how the other kids knew. Because everyone knew about the murders. Everyone knew because Mara made sure to tell them in great detail, making her notorious and a pariah all at once.

The anger dissipated, leaving her a deflated balloon. She pushed the beer away and sank into one of the chairs, cradling her hand against her body.

He brought more ice, replaced what was melting with a new wrapped dishtowel, held it to her knuckles.

His hand on her palm was so warm. Even the last time he'd been so damned warm. Hot summer day, complete meltdown volcano warm.

"Your ex is an ass." She peered up at him. "She said she's not your ex."

"I don't care what she says," he muttered. "I'm sorry she upset you."

"She didn't do this," she said fiercely. "I don't let anyone do that to me—ever."

That, he believed she believed. "You're pissed I walked away and didn't take you to bed."

"Keep thinking that."

"Why lie to me, Kayla?"

"I know all about you—what you were, what you are." She let the words tumble out fast as she stood. "I read about it."

"But all you can think about is, what if Diane was right about the way I am in bed," he challenged. "You thought about the way I held you when I kissed you. The way your body responded. You could've come so easily for me."

Damn him for being so completely right. His cheeks were flushed dark with a bristling anger that seemed to invade his whole body. He moved closer but she didn't back down, didn't stumble back in fear. "So what?"

"You're fighting me."

"I thought you liked it rough," she challenged.

"Sweetheart, you have no idea what I like. And if you think listening to Diane is the way to find out, you're really fucking wrong." He bit the words out, especially Diane's name. "I know what you're doing, even if you don't. All the fighting is to get my attention. And you've got it. But that's not enough for you—you keep pushing me to lose control. From the very first night, that's what you wanted." It was the truth. Her body stilled, belly fluttered as his voice lowered dangerously. "When I do lose control, you're not going to like it."

"You don't know that—you don't know what I like." She tugged at him fiercely, dug her nails into his skin and heat spread through him at the pinch. "Try me."

Try me.

Two simple words that could get them into such trouble.

In the past, she had pushed and somehow, she'd still retained all the control. But this time, it was so different. Maybe she'd had a vague hope that she could hold onto it this time, but one look in Teige's eyes told her that she'd lost the battle and was on her way to losing the war in spectacular fashion.

He hadn't lost any control—not yet, at least. And she'd been under the impression that he would tie her up. Spank her. Fuck her hard.

What he was doing to her was far more arousing than any of that, and harder for her to handle. She was going to like it. And she never, ever liked it. Never just gave herself over.

She'd never retain her power with Teige and he was calling her bluff.

He gave her one last out, telling her, "There's so much you don't know. So much you shouldn't ever want to."

"So why are you still here?" she challenged. "I sure as hell didn't invite you in here. You broke in. Maybe I should call the police."

With a smirk, he handed his cell phone to her, placed it in her palm and curled her fingers around it so she didn't drop it. And then he was on her, lifting her hips to the counter, a finger flicking her nipple, his mouth on her neck.

She clutched the cell phone.

"Make the call or put your hands over your head and keep them there."

The words alone could send her spiraling into an orgasm. She wanted to press her thighs together but he was already between her legs, spreading them, his crotch not touching her. She wanted to shift her hips forward, press his bulge to her sex and rub for some sweet relief.

"Call. Tell them I'm intruding." His hand slipped under her shirt. "Tell them I'm forcing you. Holding you down."

He was doing none of those things.

"Tell them you want me gone."

Not true at all.

"Tell them, or put your hands over your head," he repeated, and there was no room in his tone to say no. And so she didn't. Put the phone down with a clatter on the old countertop and slid her hands over her head, feeling foolish. Would he make fun of her? Leave her like this?

He did neither. Instead, he gazed at her, lust in his eyes, making sure she was comfortable, held her wrists in his hand and in place so they could relax.

Her head was against the cabinet, his arousal pressing between her thighs while he kissed her, hard and fast enough to take her breath away. And just when she thought she'd come then and there, he pulled back, softened his kiss and she heard herself mewl in protest.

He'd marked her neck, a possessive gesture, one that everyone could see.

His hand traveled her body. She pushed her chest in its path but he ignored it purposely, went straight for the waist of the loose sweats she wore.

His fingers slipped between her legs, found her sex, which was wet and hot for him. He stroked his fingers along her folds and she jumped, because it had been so long. Forever, it seemed, and it had never been like this.

"No more about what happened tonight. This is about us."

"What if I only want one thing from you?" she managed.

"Right now, I'll take whatever I can get."

Her legs were splayed. His fingers found her clit, a throbbing bundle of nerves that begged to be handled.

"I've never—" She shook her head, because nothing was working except her arousal. It didn't matter that she'd never. She was going to. She tried to move away, but there was nowhere to go.

She felt desperate. Hot and needed.

"I can't—not that way," she panted.

"Not this way?" he asked, his fingers still working her sex, making her hump the counter no matter how hard she tried to fight the urge.

"Come. I've never come from just this—"

It didn't matter that she'd never. She was going to. She moaned—unintelligible, Teige's name—and then nothing mattered but the gorgeous throb of a climax between her legs, the orgasm taking control of her before any more words could tumble out of her mouth, spiraling her higher and higher until the pleasure that socked her contracted through her womb.

She closed her eyes and let herself fall into it, let Teige hold her up, murmur to her that she needed to listen to him more. That she would, if he had anything to say about it.

She could. She did, even kept her hands where he told her to when he released them, holding fast to the handle of the cabinet when he let go to grab a chair and sit in front of her. When he pulled her sweats completely off, she shook her head. Like that could stop him.

He buried his head in between her legs and took her with his tongue, scraped his teeth along her too-sensitive flesh. He stared up at her and she couldn't look away, even as the orgasm began to rise inside her again.

She'd never come twice like this, never this close to each other, and she screamed out his name as the climax shook her. And still, he didn't stop.

She was practically sobbing then, but she surrendered all control to him, because it was so much easier. Because she obviously trusted him.

Because right now, she didn't want any other choice.

He wasn't done. Couldn't be. Not with Kayla so open and willing for him.

She still held the cabinet handles, but her body had gone slack and relaxed...and he planned on riling her up again. He remained between her legs, and when she opened her eyes, she gave him a soft, shy smile. Put her hand through his hair as if to smooth it, like she hadn't been just as wild and out of control moments earlier. She looked over his chest, up close and personal, her eyes cataloging the various scars scattered over his torso.

She'd ask about them later—he was sure of it.

He caressed one ankle, as her calves were still over his shoulders. He kissed the inside of her knee and she gave a wobbly smile, like she was intoxicated.

"You like ordering me."

"Yeah," he agreed, and she giggled at that. Giggled, for christsakes, and it made him smile and made his cock harden more at the same time.

And then she said, "I don't think—"

"Then don't," he told her. He licked down her inner thigh and slowly moved her legs from his shoulders. She went to close them but he stood in between them, stopping her. "My choice."

"Always?"

"It's how I like it. After tonight, you tell me if you still do."

She nodded, but was still off center. He kept a hand on her thigh to hold her in place. And then, in one motion, he scooped her into his arms and was carrying her up the stairs.

"Third floor," she told him, which was unnecessary, because he'd caught her looking at him several times when he was staring into the woods, wanting everything to return to any semblance of normalcy.

He wasn't exactly there yet either, but this was helping.

His job—his life—was violent. That was simply a matter of fact, a constant freight train, allowing himself the complete contradiction to career out of control while still retaining it whenever he took one of those black ops jobs. At one time, he'd needed that.

Would he always? Did he still?

He didn't think about his overwhelming, unshakable desire for control in his sex life. He needed that the way he needed air. He couldn't feel badly about it because it was such a part of him, as much as his sexual preference was.

He thought about the way Kayla's wrists felt in the palm of his hand, the slight resistance at first, the way she'd attempted to pull away until finally she'd allowed her body to melt against his. A show of submission, whether she realized it or not.

One thing people never seemed to realize was how strong someone needed to be in order to submit. Kayla was stronger than she gave herself credit for.

She trusts you.

He couldn't fuck that up.

In Teige's strong arms, nothing could hurt her.

Her world had been so small, and she'd hated it. Until now. With Teige, she wanted it that way, wanted it to be just about the two of them, with no space in between. Wanted his body naked in front of her, maybe even sprawled out under her submissively.

She must've been smiling wickedly as he laid her on the mattress. He gazed at her hungrily, his jeans unzipped, his arousal a hard bulge. He knew what she was thinking, had to have known what she'd been envisioning.

Other women he'd been with must've wanted the same thing. Judging by the look in his eyes, they'd never gotten it. Would she?

Do you really want that?

She couldn't answer, could only capitulate to his growled order to "Lie back on the bed and open your arms."

She was floating, and it wasn't only from the medicine. She already felt amazing and was willing to let him take her further than she'd ever gone, if only to hold on to the way her body tingled.

He slid his jeans down. "I won't tie your ankles if you follow my instructions. This time. Arms up."

Her words caught in her throat at the sight of him naked. She put her hands up. He tied them together with two T-shirts. She tugged and realized she couldn't get out of them herself, but before she could panic about that he was kissing her again, fingering her still-sensitive sex and everything inside her relaxed.

"Make me come, Teige," she murmured.

"Bossy little thing," he breathed into her ear. "You don't realize you don't have a say."

In response, she ground her pelvis against his. Begging, but she had a wicked smile on her face.

He felt lighter than he'd been in years. Decades. He bent his head and kissed her, loving the way her tongue explored his mouth. Her hands fisted, her wrists tugged their bonds even as his hand spanned both her wrists and held them fast to the mattress. Her legs were wrapped around his waist and his cock slid along her sex but she said, "Teige," and her voice halted. When he pulled back, she said, "I just..." And then she stopped, shook her head.

He watched her carefully, dreading that she might say this was too much for her. Because if this was... "Say it, Kayla."

She blurted out, "Are you doing this because you're mad at Diane?"

Relief washed over him. "If I slept with someone every time Diane made me mad, my dick would've fallen off a long time ago."

"Then why?"

"Because you took my damned picture."

And then there was no more talking. Not anything other than telling her she was *wet, hot, tight...ready for him,* how he *wanted to taste her again, make her scream his name tonight*...and the phrases spilled from him easily, but purposely to make her blush—*because I love making you blush*—and groan and grind against him.

When he put a finger inside her, she was so tight, despite how wet she was. He took his time opening her, not wanting anything to ruin this. She didn't take her eyes off him, which made everything that much hotter.

When he added a second finger, her eyes widened and her mouth formed a small O. He took her nipple between his teeth, held it there lightly and listened as her breathing quickened.

With his tongue, he began tracing wet paths down her body, swiping her nipples then ignoring them, leaving her whimpering for more.

"You want more, little one, don't you," he murmured and she bit her bottom lip to keep from crying out again. She couldn't control her pulse or her breathing, and he smiled as he watched her losing all sense of control.

She was vaguely aware of the rip of the foil package of a condom and realized with a start that she'd been so far gone it wouldn't have been a thought in her mind.

But Teige—he had it all under control. It made her able to lose it that much more easily.

And then, before she could form any further coherent thoughts, he flexed his hips, pushing inside her, and her breath caught, stuttered and she cried out. He stilled for just a moment and then he began fucking her, taking her the way he'd wanted to from the first night he'd met her. And she let him, opened herself to him as he closed his eyes, as he struggled to remain in control of his orgasm. But Kayla bucked her hips, her wet heat sucking him in, milking him until his climax ripped from him. He was aware that he called out her name, his voice hoarse, his chest heaving as she took him as much—and as hard—as he took her.

Chapter 13

SHE'D BEEN ABUSED. Teige stared hard at the bottoms of Kayla's feet where the long-healed scars of cigarette burns scattered along the arch.

The bastard who did it made sure they were well hidden. Were there others he missed? He'd been over her body all night and he was always observant. His mind tugged him to the spot on her inner thigh he'd assumed was a birthmark by touch. Now, fingering the bottom of her foot as she slept, he knew better.

But she slept. At night. He knew this was probably something of a minor miracle, based on her habits and her own admissions, and maybe he'd just discovered the whys.

She didn't act like a child abuse survivor—didn't mind being held down and controlled—and she hadn't done it just to please him. He knew better.

This had all gotten so much more complicated. And maybe it was the right time, the perfect storm. He felt better than he had in years, like he could actually curl around her and sleep.

But he would keep watch while she did so. Think about what to say when she woke.

He'd found the book that someone lent her, a copy dog-eared on the pages that centered around him and his missions. He hadn't read it himself but he could only imagine what was written. All true, and probably watered down, since the missions were still classified.

He'd avoided the movie version because he'd lived it. Wasn't sure how to feel about having his name touted as one of the greatest Special Forces Operators. He took his job seriously. Had saved a lot of people, but he sure in hell hadn't done it for the small burst of glory the publicity had afforded him.

His town had gathered around him, protected him from press. But his locale, his face, everything was still shrouded in secrecy, so no reporters ever came to him. For that, he was grateful.

"You're thinking loudly."

She was staring up at him, an arm tucked under her head, the sheet barely covering her.

"Sorry."

She glanced over to the night table. "I guess I shouldn't have read that."

"No rule saying you can't."

"It upsets you."

"Sometimes," he agreed, and decided not to ask her about the abuse. Not tonight. Maybe not ever.

Maybe she'll bring it up to me when she's comfortable. Although she looks decidedly so.

"Were you kicked out of the Army?"

"No, I took retirement early on the strong rec of the shrink. I think it had something to do with me saying I wanted to kill every motherfucker out there."

"You did that on purpose."

He shrugged. "I needed out. Better that I was on my own. I could do less damage that way."

"I do know what you mean." In the moonlight, Kayla's eyes glowed, a little wet, but she didn't seem exactly sad. "This is the first time I've been in the dark in forever."

He took pride in that. "Dark's not so bad."

"It's not, now that my eyes have finally adjusted."

"You can gain a big advantage in the dark," Teige told her.

"You already took that advantage."

"Yeah, that's not what I'm talking about."

"I didn't say I minded."

It was what he'd been hoping to hear. She didn't appear to have any regrets, but he'd know more next time he came to town.

"Why did you stay with Diane for so long?" she asked now.

"I don't know. She's not a bad person. We're bad for each other."

"She's bad. You're punishing yourself by being with her," she said.

Could it really be that simple, he wondered. Maybe Diane was punishing herself too. He didn't know much about her past, because she refused to talk about it. She never wanted gentle and he never thought himself capable of it, but maybe he was. Kayla seemed to bring it out in him, even as she sought his dominance.

She would push him to his limits, even as she explored hers. That excited him, more than he'd been in years.

"How, Teige?" she asked quietly. "How did you know what I'd want?"

"I knew what you needed. It might not always be what you want. Sometimes, it's in direct opposition." He stroked a finger under her chin and she shivered at his touch. "Giving up control doesn't make you weak. It's the opposite, really, but most don't ever understand that. You do."

Kayla lay next to him, rubbed her wrists, not wanting to admit she liked the way the red marks looked on them and realizing she just had. She blushed when she thought about the way he'd tied her. The way she'd screamed for him.

The way she'd had such a completely out-of-body experience after coming three times in the space of an hour. "I wish you didn't have to leave again."

She wanted to ask where he was going, how long he'd be gone. Wanted to know if maybe, this time, he could stay in touch.

God damn, she was needy. Instead of saying anything, she curled her hand around his forearm, feeling the rope of muscles strong under her touch. He was watching her, waiting for her to say something and when she didn't, he said, "You don't mind watching Hanny again?"

"Never."

That got a soft smile from him. "She likes you. A lot."

"Can you stay for a while?"

"I leave at o-dark hundred. Which means I need to get going. Can you go back to sleep?"

"I'd need you here for that."

He started at that but he didn't pull away from her. She wondered if she'd ever be able to control her words around him and decided no, that she was decidedly out of control in his presence.

———

She heard Teige's truck start, and so did Hanny, who jumped up and watched out the window. Kayla waited until Hanny came back to her and curled around her legs protectively.

They'd had more sex—much more—after a quick and frank discussion when they were both panting with need, about how often he was tested...and how long it had been since she'd been with anyone. About how she was on the pill anyway, for many different reasons unrelated to sex, like the migraines. And they'd done away with the condoms.

She waited an hour before finally calling Abby, unable to avoid it any longer.

When Abby answered, Kayla simply asked, "Who was she?"

A pause, and then, "A juror. From the original trial."

"How would Mara find that out?" she demanded.

"She shouldn't be able to," Abby admitted.

But that had never stopped her before. Nothing stopped Mara. And there was no way this was a coincidence. "There's something else you're not telling me."

"There's a second female juror missing."

She rubbed her arms. Couldn't tell if the original feeling about Mara was centered on both women or not. She wasn't sure what terrified her more—the fact that she was possibly losing her bond with Mara...or that she wouldn't ever lose it. "You weren't supposed to give me that information."

"You're right."

"So why did you?"

"I think you have a right to know," Abby said simply.

'Thank you' seemed the wrong response so Kayla nodded, like Abby could see her.

Chapter 14

ABBY CAUGHT some sleep on the cot in the back room, woke around four in the morning, showered and put on fresh clothes she always kept in her locker. Hair still wet on her shoulders, she grabbed some coffee from a fresh pot the night staff made, sugared it enough to keep her flying for hours and checked her phone and email for the millionth time.

Nothing from Ethan.

Nothing from Kayla.

She couldn't help but wonder if nothing was better than a something she didn't want to hear. She'd learned that no news was good news, but that didn't necessarily apply in Ethan's case. And maybe not in Kayla's either.

She threaded through the office, noting that the skeleton crew was winding down. Finishing up paperwork. Music played softly from one corner of the room and most used desk lamps, opting to turn off the harsh fluorescents above.

Nighttime here had a whole different rhythm to it.

These days, no one asked Abby if she ever went home —she appreciated that the teasing had stopped. They seemed to respect that she was this devoted to her job. At least that's what she told herself. In reality they probably felt sorry for her and she couldn't face that.

But she also couldn't change it. There was no time off for Abby. Hadn't been as long as she'd made this job her life.

She rifled through her desk, finding the familiar paper enclosed in the evidence baggie. It was supposed to be in the folder, but she wouldn't place it there until the case had been closed.

The note she held now had come in an hour before the phone call, too late for her to make any connection.

Hoss. I like the name. He seemed nice. Claire liked him. And he ended up liking me...really liking me.

Killing him was easy. He didn't see it coming. Didn't recognize me. Crazy, right? How could he not recognize me?

I don't want to kill. I have to. Claire knows it too. She can feel it when it's too much for me. Ask her...I know she felt this one.

She had.

Abby put the baggie back into the drawer—it had already been vetted for fingerprints. Mara hadn't bothered to hide them.

She sipped her coffee as she stared at a map of the city where the juror's body had been found. Did that until the sound of the security beep made her look up.

Someone was coming through the door. She saw the flash of a badge and figured it had to be her new partner.

At first she thought he was early, and then realized that hours had passed and it was nearly eight. She'd lost track of time, allowed morning to sneak up on her.

He was dressed in all black—jeans, T-shirt under a leather jacket that looked worn enough to tell her he was the real deal in it, not just a poser. The black, heavy motorcycle boots confirmed the sounds of a loud motorcycle that'd pulled up outside moments before he'd walked in. No helmet, unless he'd left it outside.

Instead, he carried a small, zippered case that looked like it held no more than a laptop and some files.

Lena, the secretary, was flirting with him. Abby could tell by the tilt of the woman's head, but Jacoby Razwell was already staring over Lena's shoulder directly at Abby.

"Maybe because you're staring him down," she muttered, brushing through her air-dried hair with her fingers self-consciously. She took a sip of her coffee, refusing now to stop looking just because she'd been caught.

He had messy, dark hair, dark eyes. Brooding. Like a goddamned rock star instead of a US Marshal and maybe she should've done some kind of background check on him. She'd wanted to give him the benefit of the doubt, she told herself.

In truth, she figured since he'd only been with the

marshals for a year, he was too new for him to be anything but the fucking new guy.

Lena turned and pointed toward Abby. Jacoby nodded at Lena and walked in a missile-straight line toward Abby, who remained with her ass perched half on the corner of her desk as she finished her third cup of coffee of the morning.

He extended a hand and she took it and gave a firm shake. "Abby Daniels."

He opened his mouth to introduce himself but "Hey, Raz," came from behind him and Clive was patting him on the back. "Didn't think we'd see you in this office—you were headed for the big time."

"Big time's not all it's cut out to be," was Raz's answer, his voice low and gravelly, a smoker's voice, although he smelled like fresh air instead, and Abby tucked that information about the big time away carefully.

Who the hell had they paired her with—someone who'd been kicked out of the main offices?

He didn't seem all that concerned she'd heard the exchange. His expression remained placid as he looked between her and Clive, and Clive talked a little about how the office ran and Abby's experience.

"I've heard nothing but good things about Marshal Daniels," Jacoby said and she gave a curt nod. She wasn't going to give him an inch—not yet.

Everyone had something to prove. She needed to see just how much—and how far—Jacoby Razwell was willing to go.

"I've read up on our witness," he said, pulling out a

folder and a small laptop from the bag. "Any leads on Mara?"

"The last killing took place in Arizona. She could be anywhere. Never kills in the same county, never mind state."

"How's she supporting herself?" Jacoby's question seemed more like he was talking to himself than to her, but it was something she'd often asked herself.

"We're suspecting she's using stolen social security numbers to collect disability or get jobs."

He considered that for a moment. "Maybe she's running scams on men."

"She's pretty enough—but also notorious."

"Maybe it's part of the thrill."

She considered that, then reminded him, "It's our job to keep the witness safe, not profile Mara."

"And that's why you're looking at a map of the county Mara was last spotted in."

"Touché," she muttered. "It's been a long time since I had a partner."

"And you didn't want a new one. I figured that. Have you looked me up already or are you going to hear it from me first?"

She pointed to her computer. "Want to check my search history?"

But Jacoby was suddenly more interested in his phone. "You might want to make your check-ins on your witness a little more thorough. She punched a local," he informed her.

"Wait, what?" Abby demanded. "And why's she only *my* witness?"

"When she does shit wrong, she's mine?" Jacoby asked and Abby nodded. He sighed. "She hit a local—some chick named Diane."

Abby groaned. She'd heard Teige alternately bitch and moan about Diane more times than she cared to remember. She guessed that Diane tried to make a police report...and that it got kicked right through to the marshals' office.

"Think we need to pay her a visit?" Jacoby continued.

"Which one?"

"Your witness."

Abby rolled her eyes. "She checked in. An 'okay' test an hour ago."

"And the police report was filed about a minute later. I called the station and made sure there was no meet and greet, but Diane wants a restraining order."

Shit. What the hell had Kayla been thinking?

"Has Kayla seen a therapist?"

"Yes, when she was first in protection. A little more with Hoss, but not lately. It's not unlike Kayla to fight, though. She wasn't exactly a model teen."

"Right." Jacoby frowned. "On paper, she looked way more like the candidate most likely to commit a violent act."

"Can't judge a book," she said hollowly, her fingers brushing across her iPad to find no check-in from Ethan. The disappointment must've shown clearly on her face, because Jacoby asked, "Waiting for news?"

"It's all I do."

"Sounds like you resent it."

She glanced up at him. "You won't get an argument from me."

Jacoby motioned to the iPad. "Come on—you haven't eaten yet. Let's grab some breakfast."

"I—"

"We're partners. Getting to know each other is imperative."

He left no room for further argument.

The newest job wasn't driving supplies through IED-ridden land, which was a combination of Russian roulette meets Frogger. No, this one concerned getting a businessman out of the hands of Mexican kidnappers. It was pretty much the national business, second only to drug dealing.

And even though Teige had already extracted the businessman—Dale Harrison—and killed the guards quietly enough, getting Dale out of Mexico would prove to be more difficult. It would require at least a week, if not more, of hiding in safe houses, letting things die down before smuggling him back out of the country. The guy was a billionaire and the kidnappers wanted their money—and if they couldn't have their money, they'd use the guy's dead body as a warning to other businessmen that they weren't fooling around. To top it off, they had contacts at the border, which meant an illegal exit was also in the cards.

Nothing in this place was safe—everyone could be

bought for the right price, although Teige supposed he could say that about anywhere.

That hit home harder when he'd stumbled back to the waiting truck with Dale and discovered that Kirby—former Army Ranger and his lookout—had been shot and killed. Most likely a robbery and nothing to do with the kidnapping. But it necessitated wrapping Kirby up and putting his body in the back—Teige would find a place to bury him, because hell, he couldn't take a dead body across the border. His boss would have to send someone in to retrieve it.

He said a short prayer before he loaded Kirby into the back of the truck. It shouldn't have mattered, but it always would. He didn't want to cop to the fact that it was just possible that his whole career was based on a lie—the fact that he could turn his emotions off, that he believed war wasn't personal.

Tonight, for the first time, he admitted that he knew better.

He leaned into the passenger's side window to check on Dale. The guy'd pissed his pants, and Teige pretended not to notice. But once they parked, he clapped a hand on Dale's shoulder to move him forward, spilling a bottle of water across both their laps so no one would know. Both of them smelled to high heaven anyway. Dale'd been captured for four days, held in a stifling cell, and Teige spent the better part of two days lying in the same position, waiting for his break.

This was his last black ops job. Maybe he wouldn't

stick to that internal proclamation, but at this moment he truly fucking believed it.

He was done. He'd find something mindless to do, like train future Deltas or bodyguard. Anything but this merc-for-hire shit. It was killing him. Maybe it always had and he hadn't realized it.

Maybe he was just like his goddamned father.

He'd grown up with an odd sense of violence—it was all around him, the periphery of his life—but it hadn't touched him. Yet. The statistics were there. He watched his father investigate horrific things and knew it was only a matter of time before the claws of something dark and deep reached out to harm his family, no matter how much Mom tried to cocoon them.

But after she died, the violence consumed their father and overwhelmed Teige to the point where he knew he had no choice but to jump in and swim. For years he did, immersed himself in his father's work, let the violence batter him from the inside out until he was bleeding. Raw and vulnerable.

He knew that if he didn't drag himself away, he'd drown. His father was sinking into the abyss and had refused Teige's hand to help him climb out.

That obsession had killed him as sure as another man's hands. By then, Teige was already ensconced in the Army, through Ranger school and in the process of being considered for Delta Force training, although he hadn't known that at the time. Thankfully, he'd had that to sink into with a single-minded drive that got him through the grief and rage, lasering his focus sharp and narrow.

Delta saved him—and he'd needed saving.

But his mother's words still rang in his ears. *You have to use the gifts you've been given.*

He'd ignored her successfully...until now.

Abby drove to the diner—Jacoby opted to go with her instead of on his bike, which meant she didn't even have those few minutes to pull herself together. She turned the radio up so she didn't have to talk and he didn't try.

She took her usual booth in the back, with the usual waitress, and realized that her life had become completely routine over the past month. She'd relocated here first while Kayla was watched in a locked-down safe house. Abby's apartment was two towns over—close enough to get to Kayla fast but not too close so that people connected her and Kayla together.

It was always such a balancing act, and she was doing a good impression of vertigo at the moment. She studied the menu, stealing glances at the iPad she'd parked next to it. Hoping Ethan would get back in touch but knowing she wouldn't hear from him again for days.

The constant worry from that balled in her gut, but she had to eat. She ordered a burger and fries—her new usual—and caught sight of two young boys sitting side by side, sipping milkshakes and sharing secrets in the way boys did. Quiet. So quiet you'd think they weren't talking at all.

One of them had a black eye. She wondered if the friend defended him. Her thoughts pulled her back to

Teige. Age nine. On the playground, defending an unpopular boy against bullies. Standing up for those who couldn't stand up for themselves. Not caring how many people turned against him.

It almost seemed like he wanted it that way. Then he could remain alone. Unbothered.

Helping the weak, being left alone—a good deed leading to exactly what he wanted.

Abby scratched an itch on her elbow, caught Jacoby looking at her. She'd decided she'd call him Jacoby because it would annoy a man who wanted to be called Raz. "Where are you staying, Jacoby?"

He didn't look annoyed, but rather pleased—a cocky pleased. Pleased like she's-been-thinking-about-me pleased.

You fucked up. "Or would you rather I call you Raz?"

"Right now, I'm at the Hilton. And I prefer Jacoby."

"Then why let them call you Raz?"

"I pick my battles. That's not one of them."

That she understood. She turned the iPad in a circle with an index finger, praying it would flash on, that Ethan would explain more

Jacoby noticed. "You keep looking at the iPad. Expecting an email?"

"Not exactly. Friend of mine's in a war zone."

"Sorry."

She wanted to say, "He's fine" or "Don't be" in that hurried way you say things when you really want to say, "I'm scared to death."

Instead, she said, "Thanks" as the waitress put their

food down. Jacoby shrugged out of his jacket and push the sleeves of his T-shirt up slightly, but enough to reveal the intricate bands of what looked like tribal ink tattoos.

"How long?" Jacoby asked when they were alone again.

Abby stopped looking at his arms and concentrated instead on squeezing the ketchup onto her plate like it was the most important job in the world before saying, "Six months, give or take a few days."

She had the exact count in her head, but she wasn't telling him that.

"Shit." Jacoby turned the mug around inside his palms.

"Yeah, shit," she echoed. "Any ideas about Mara?"

"Just got the case yesterday. I know the main details, but not enough to work up to a theory beyond trying to fuck her sister over any way she can."

"Yeah, Mara loves her to death," she muttered.

"You think she's waiting for Kayla to join her?" Jacoby asked.

"It's not out of the realm of possibility. But I also don't accept Mara as a true serial killer," Abby told him.

"She presents as one. Mara's killing to get Kayla's attention. To get our attention."

"But most serial killers do kill that one trigger when they have the chance. Usually one of their first kills," Abby pointed out. "And she was in close enough physical proximity to Kayla for years."

Jacoby shrugged. "Guess we'll have to ask her when we catch her. Do you believe Kayla's innocent?"

Abby dipped a fry in ketchup. "I'm charged with protecting her. My beliefs don't matter."

"Not what I asked." Jacoby played with his coffee mug until she put a hand out to stop him from spinning it.

"I don't know."

"Me neither. And I can't imagine her living with that constant suspicion if she's innocent."

If.

Her phone began to beep and she stared down at the text from their boss. "Autopsy on the juror's back."

"Rain check." Jacoby threw down money to cover their tab, and the waitress was already at the table with to-go Styrofoam for them. Abby ate her burger as she drove them back to the office for a briefing, realizing she'd gone five minutes without thinking about Ethan.

Progress, she supposed.

Chapter 15

ABBY CALLED her daily after giving her the news that a second juror had gone missing, even though there were no new leads. The rest of the men and women from that particular jury pool were all present and accounted for, so Kayla tried to keep some semblance of normal going, taking Hanny for long walks in the park and the like.

It had been nearly three weeks since Teige left. At one point, Penny called to check on her and when she heard Hanny in the background, she commented, "Guess your soldier's away."

She wanted to say, "He's not mine" but the words wouldn't come out. Instead, she told Penny, "He's gone longer than he said."

"They can't give exact times. The thing is, Kayla, if something was really wrong, you'd probably know about it already. That's one of the lessons I learned of military life."

If something was really wrong, you'd probably know about it already. Penny didn't know how true those words rang, but Kayla found herself sitting on the floor, rubbing her arms.

Someone's walking on your grave.

"God, no," she whispered. Hadn't felt Mara's presence this strongly since...

Since Hoss.

There was nothing else for her to do but wait to hear from Abby. It might be an hour from now or several days, but a call would come and it would be to tell her they found the second juror. In the meantime, Kayla holed up in the house, going out to walk Hanny midday, gun concealed under her jacket, and that was it. She refused Penny's invites, didn't go to the diner or over to Mrs. Mueller's.

Finally, on the thirty-second day that Teige was away, Abby called.

"We found the second juror," she said without preamble. Kayla appreciated the non-coddling.

"Where?"

"California, near San Leandro. Another cemetery. Looks like it happened in the last twenty-four hours."

Kayla sank to the couch, said a quick thank you it happened on the other side of the country and immediately felt guilty. "This is definitely her."

"We believe so, yes. We're monitoring it closely, Kayla. You're safe where you are. Just stay close to the town, do what you're doing."

"The press?"

"Is keeping this quiet. The other jurors are being

contacted. Put into temporary protection," Abby explained.

"Why now?"

"I wish I could answer that."

"Me too," she said absently, waited until Abby hung up before she did.

Don't think, don't think, don't think.

It's been six months.

That means nothing.

The creaking upstairs, the moving chair once she got up there, was oddly reassuring.

"It's escalating. *She's* escalating," she said out loud.

Kayla would work herself into a self-pitying, complete frenzy if she continued like this. She looked at the bottle of Jack Daniels Teige had left her, wondered if that kind of self-medication was warranted or wise.

Probably a little of both. She drank a shot glass full of the stuff and allowed herself to try to remember.

She barely recalled the faces of the jurors, had never known their names. If she and Mara hadn't looked exactly alike, maybe Kayla would've been able to exact more pity from them. Or maybe that was her own guilty conscience. Either way, by the third day of her testimony she'd stopped looking in their direction, no matter how many times her lawyer admonished her for not doing so.

It was a horrible time, but Kayla had been relieved that Mara would be put away for a long time. Mara admitted she was the one to commit the crimes...with the caveat that it was because of Kayla. And that Kayla was a murderer too.

That had changed everything, especially the mood of the trial and the tone of the press. There would always be doubt and suspicion.

And they had no idea their service would cost them their lives. Abby swore that now they were all being contacted and placed under protection. But what kind of life would that be? Some would refuse, and until Mara was stopped—or died—none of their lives would continue as they should.

Twelve jurors and two alternates. Fourteen was down to twelve. No one could figure out how Mara got those names, but Kayla could see Mara holding on to that information for years, patiently waiting until it was the right time.

Could her twin even feel love? The psych profiles made that seem like a slim-to-none possibility. And that made Kayla sadder than anything, meant there wasn't a chance that Mara could be saved.

If Kayla made a public plea for her, if she asked Mara to come back...

If she admitted to a crime she hadn't committed...

What would that bring her? The public would come down on her, but if Kayla could get Mara off the street, would any of that matter?

Mara's body count was up to ten. Ten that they knew of. More women than men, but the BAU simply surmised that women were easier for Mara to subdue, at least physically.

To this day, she could hear Mara telling the police that the man she'd seen was big, with funny drawings on his arms. When they'd asked her to draw the symbols, she'd drawn a swastika. A meth-selling white supremacist.

They'd brought in suspects, but Mara couldn't identify any of them, so nothing ever stuck.

"But why wouldn't Mara go after white supremacists?" she remembered asking, because it never made sense.

"Her eight-year-old mind was irrevocably altered," they explained to her patiently. Mara was disturbed. Not rational at all.

From the trial, she remembered hearing bits and pieces of Mara's psychology. "Love map—established by the age of six...Mara's was obviously corrupted by that point."

As was yours. You're just lucky you can't remember.

There were times she wished she did. It would make things easier, simpler.

She tensed when she heard Hanny's bark. The dog ran up the stairs to her and then went over to the window.

"Teige's back," she whispered to herself. He could protect her. "No, you can't think like that," she lectured herself. "You can't think beyond yourself."

She was too involved. Expecting too much. She knelt down and rubbed her hands in Hanny's fur. In return, the dog burrowed against her and she knew she'd sleep because of this gentle giant.

"Your dad will come for you soon," she assured her. How she'd gotten this close to Teige should've surprised her, but after knowing him for five minutes it didn't. He was so completely right for her, no matter how wrong she was for everyone.

Her ex hadn't been right for her—she'd known it, as had

Hoss. In fact, that's when Hoss started getting close to her in a way that made Kayla slightly uncomfortable...at first. When Kayla did finally attempt to give in to his flirting a few months later, he was strangely hands-off. And after Hoss's death, the marshals spirited her away quietly, under the cover of darkness, and she'd never thought to mention that Hoss had tried to sleep with her. She'd assumed it happened more often than not, since she couldn't imagine having a long-term relationship while in WITSEC. She'd been told that there might be times she'd have to leave her new place, new town, new name behind without so much as an explanation. Because how could she ever trust someone to understand, much less keep her secrets?

She hadn't...until Teige.

She'd thought she'd had enough excitement in her life...enough upheaval that safe and boring would feel right. But that had been all wrong.

Weeks of excruciating silence. Each day, the tension got worse. Abby's sleep was restless at best, and she'd survived by eating greasy food and downing coffee solely to stay awake and keep moving. She had constant contact with Kayla, who was taking Teige's extended absence hard.

Abby didn't know if that was good or bad.

"Jurors are all good," Jacoby reported now. He'd taken on the task of letting the marshals guarding each of the remaining ones check in with him three times a day.

"She's too quiet."

"She's definitely not dormant—no chance of that happening. If anything, I'd expect her to be escalating," Jacoby mused.

He was definitely profiling, but Abby recognized it was necessary—at this point, guarding Kayla wasn't enough. Anticipating Mara's next move, in conjunction with the FBI, was.

At the start of this, Abby didn't want constant contact with the FBI. Now, she didn't have much choice. It was once again the most active of investigations, with a new team, a new profiler on the case. The old one had died of a heart attack years ago, so they were starting from scratch with his notes and Kayla's help.

Which Kayla wouldn't really give them.

Thankfully, Jacoby was running point with the FBI team, leaving her to be Kayla's constant contact.

"Best not to make too many changes on her now. You know her best," Jacoby had said and Abby was only too happy to agree.

Kayla had been actively refusing to have Abby stay with her, or to be assigned a 24/7 detail. Abby and her supervisor had agreed that it might call too much attention to Kayla and her status with the town...

As for Mara knowing where Kayla was, Abby felt the only way that would happen was if Kayla was actually speaking with Mara.

Which she wasn't, as far as any of them knew.

"Trail's gone cold," Jacoby told her after he hung up

with the FBI. "No leads. Nothing. She's really covering her tracks."

"How do you know she hasn't gone dormant? It's happened before."

"I wish, Abby. I think we have to concentrate on other avenues."

"Like?"

"Mara's got to have help," Jacoby said, frowning at the case files he'd been paging through.

"Now who's profiling?" She caught a fleeting expression on his face that told her profiling was a more personal thing than he was letting on.

"Everyone's got to do their part, right?" he offered by way of explanation before continuing to sift through Mara's records. "Any way Mara could've turned Hoss?"

"Never." She must've hissed the word, because Jacoby put his hands up in silent surrender. "Sorry, but to even consider that..."

"Consider it," he ordered firmly. "Females who kill can be more charming than their male counterparts."

Abby managed, "Suppose he didn't know?"

"What, he falls for Kayla, and then Mara comes on to him and he doesn't realize the difference?" He shook his head at the theory. "My bet's on Mara convincing Hoss of her innocence."

Abby didn't want to consider that. It was too horrifying to think that Mara could break a man like Hoss. "If she can get to him..."

"He's not unique," Jacoby said shortly. "Men are easily swayed by a beautiful woman in jeopardy."

"And women aren't?"

"I'm admitting that, as a whole, women are the smarter sex and you're arguing with me?"

She sighed. "So Mara's been seducing marshals?"

"And lawyers. Guards at the hospitals. Kayla herself admitted that Mara was the one who made friends far more easily. That people were naturally drawn to her. Hell, Kayla faces almost the same, if not more suspicion, as Mara did. I swear, with a little more time, Mara could've convinced a jury to put Kayla in jail and walk free herself. Why everyone's been underestimating her's beyond me." Jacoby muttered that last part under his breath.

"Well thank God you've finally arrived to save us all," she shot back.

"Touchy. And technically you just caught this case. Why're you so invested?"

"You've got your skeletons, and I've got mine." He got up then and pointed toward the coffee machine on the other side of the office space. She shook her head and watched his back retreat for a second.

Did he really not know about her whole past?

Before he came back, she quickly ran Jacoby's name through the database.

Nothing.

She went to Google instead.

Nothing.

Not totally uncommon...but he should show up in the department's files. Of course, anything more than a cursory search would flag her for doing so. She might even be flagged now, but most marshals and law enforcement took a gander at their new partner's background, to know what they'd be getting into.

"Just ask him," she told herself, before letting her gaze fall to Mara's files. It was getting dangerous for her, because she'd let herself get pulled in, and she'd sworn to herself, to Teige, that she wouldn't. All for her own good, and she knew that. She'd survived something terrible. She was lucky to not be more scarred than she was, inside and out.

When he came back to the files, he sat on the edge of her desk. She turned her laptop to him so he could see the search screen with zero results.

He raised his brows but managed not to look concerned. "That's all I'm worth? A free search? What, no background check?"

"I didn't want to do any of this. Not at first."

"And now you've tried. Figured out I don't exist. So you've got all these theories running around in your head now," he said. "I'm in witness protection. I killed the real guy and I'm actually a criminal."

"You're not going to tell me, are you?"

"No. This is way more fun."

Chapter 16

THERE WAS a fire in the brick pit in Teige's backyard. At least Kayla thought there was, since it was covered.

Which meant one thing—Teige was home. Finally home.

As she watched out the window, he came out of the woods and took the cover off the fire. Then he sat back in that familiar spot and watched the smoke rise in thick puffs toward the night sky, never taking his eyes away.

She wanted to be closer to him, to see his face, the fire reflected in his eyes, the light sheen of sweat that slicked his body.

She wanted to take a picture of him so badly she ached, but instead committed the moment to memory. And she held out going to him until three in the morning. Waited until he returned from another long run in the woods and watched him sit on his porch, as she had before.

He must feel you watching.

And rather than stalk him through a window, she wanted to be face to face with him. To touch him. She let Hanny out and followed her out into the pouring rain. The dog ran to Teige, who petted her absently. He refused to meet Kayla's eyes, like if he pretended he couldn't see her, she didn't exist.

Kayla knew how that went. And still, she pushed forward until she was standing right in front of him, impossible to ignore. Taunting a sleeping beast, although that was the last thing she wanted to do.

Bullshit. You want him any way you can have him.

She'd never felt an attraction like this—it was as if they each held an end of an electrical wire and it was sizzling with live energy. Nothing—no one—had come close to touching her like this. She wanted to crawl inside his window, let him inside her until they were wild with abandon.

That total loss of control...she could never let that happen. If she stayed around Teige for any length of time, she knew she wouldn't be able to stop it.

Before she had a chance to speak, he told her gruffly, "I don't want company."

"I'm sorry. I didn't mean...Hanny missed you." *I did too. I was worried.*

Thankfully, those last thoughts didn't come out. Instead, she croaked another sorry and turned to leave, telling herself that this was all a mistake. Prepared to go inside and pack up and be out of here within the hour.

He caught her when she was halfway to her porch.

Turned her around by force and she told him furiously, "You didn't want company."

"Still don't," was his answer and she didn't know what kind of battle was raging behind his eyes. Didn't know if she should be scared of it or not, but she was so tired of fear, of looking over her shoulder, of her whole life being a ticking time bomb.

He ordered Hanny inside her house, and Hanny listened.

Then he turned his full attention to her, wrapped an arm around her waist and lifted her as if she weighed nothing at all. She wrapped her legs around his waist as he hoisted her, and still, the rain fell harder. Her shirt clung to her and he sucked one of her nipples through the wet cotton of her T-shirt, hard enough for her to feel the jolt to her womb.

Her hands twisted in his wet hair. He sucked harder, then ripped at her shirt until it tore. The wetness hit her nipples as she rode against him. She was thinking how much she missed him, or maybe she was telling him out loud as her sex spasmed. His hands were everywhere, it seemed, in the frenzy.

She let him strip her in the rain, until she was completely naked and clinging to him. He remained dressed, his jeans undone and pushed to his hips.

"I don't want this," he kept repeating, but he was lying, she supposed, because he did want her, judging by how hard he was when he entered her, pressed her against the porch rail, her ass balanced on the rough wood, protected by a T-shirt he'd slapped on there.

He smelled like the jungle, like gunpowder and battle and victory.

He smelled like danger, she thought as she buried her head against his neck as she came.

Chapter 17

AFTERWARD, he sat on the edge of the old claw-footed tub and let her wash him while he stared straight ahead. She didn't care that she was half naked, soaked to the skin. Right now, getting Teige back was most important, and not because she needed him.

Because he needs you.

He wasn't all there but she refused to let him go. She washed the dirt from his face, neck and chest, used another to wash his arousal, still hard. Then she moved down to his feet, washed them almost reverently. They were bruised in places, like the rest of him, and she worked the knotted muscles in his calves with her hands until she heard a groan of appreciation.

"I want to take care of you," she told him.

"That's a dangerous road to travel."

"I know. Damn you for it," she whispered. Wanted to freeze the night just like this so nothing at all would change, so no one would have to move forward from this moment. So she'd never have to attempt to explain something she wasn't allowed to in the first place.

But for tonight, he was more fucked up of the two of them. She'd do what she could to make it right.

Finally, he stood and wrapped wound a warm towel around her. She hadn't realized she was shivering until he did so.

"Thanks," she said softly. Liked the way his eyes glowed. There was desire there, as well as purpose.

He pulled her to him, held her there, her cheek to his chest. His heart beat so fast—she'd never have believed it from his calm facade. But they remained like that, rocking slightly, dancing to a rhythm only the two of them could hear. Her palms splayed against his bare back, feeling the old scars. His broad forearms rested on her lower back, his cock pressing her belly.

The urgency began to rise then. It was never not there, but this intensity went somehow from zero to sixty, and his mouth came down on hers as soon as she tilted her head up to him. He lifted her, and her hands went to his shoulders, her legs around his waist. Soft moans escaped their mouths—frustrated groans drummed in the back of his throat like the low growls of a stalking lion.

He wanted nothing more than to push inside her, no words, not dealing with anything beyond fucking.

But this had gone so far beyond fucking. So he pulled back, put her feet on the floor and put some space between them for a second so he could goddamned think without his cock getting in the way.

"I'm not..." He paused, wasn't sure of what to say. "I'm not..." he tried again and she put her finger to his lips.

"I'm okay enough right now for both of us."

It was what he needed to hear. He put his mouth on hers again hungrily, drawing strength from her as she'd offered it. It was all he could do not to take her right there against the sink, on the tile floor, but that was too barbaric for his tastes right now. It would take him over the edge, and he needed to remember the woman who was with him, who was edging down between his legs to take him into her mouth, who was fucking him with teeth and tongue...who was threatening to make him forget everything else existed.

He twisted a hand in her hair to hold her there and she moaned when he did. Smiled around his cock and sweet Jesus Christ, it was all too much. His bare toes curled on the cold tile floor, her fingers dug into his hip, her free hand alternately cupping his balls and stroking his shaft. He put a hand out to the wall for support, because his knees felt ready to buckle as the orgasm approached.

He wanted to put it off forever, to keep this intense, nearly painful state to remind him that he was alive, that things were okay. That he'd gotten through.

But she moaned then and the hum sent him over the edge as he spilled into her mouth.

He didn't remember her standing and leading him to the bedroom. He was lost in the hazy afterglow when even the slightest touch to his skin made him shiver.

She pushed him a little toward the bed and he didn't argue. Lay on his back and she lay down on top of him, her now naked body covering his. She planted small kisses along his collarbone as the rain began to fall in heavy sheets outside, the flashes of lightning interspersing with booms of thunder large enough to make Hanny pace restlessly in the hall outside the bedroom.

The door was open, but Hanny always stood guard in the hallway. Hanny, and the ghost of Old Man Kennen.

Neither seemed to mind the other.

Finally, he lifted a hand, smoothed her hair from her face. "Thank you."

"When I'm with you, everything melts away. It's what I need," she told him. It was exactly the way he felt with her, put so easily into words.

"Thanks for taking care of Hanny," he said, because he didn't trust himself to say anything further.

"I meant it when I said you were beautiful. And I don't just mean here." She cupped his face in her palms and then moved one down to his chest. "I meant here." A palm, flat against his heart. "My camera doesn't lie."

"Jesus, I don't fucking deserve this," was all he could say.

She leaned in and kissed him then. This time, she was the one holding his wrists to the sides. He could break the hold at any time—they both knew that. But he didn't.

She cocked her head and stared at him for a long moment. "You're leaving again soon."

"Now you're psychic?"

"I'm beginning to read you."

"Then I'm in trouble." He was only half kidding. "I leave tomorrow. I'd say it wasn't my choice, but it is."

"Because things are intense here."

"Maybe." In truth, he was like a pinball, bouncing back and forth between dangerous situations, each one intensifying the next. That was his comfort level and this—whatever was happening with Kayla—was so far out of it, he was starting to spin. Getting out would put him back in a familiar situation, one he knew how to handle.

You're running, Teige.

He told himself to fuck off.

Kayla wasn't going to be that easy to deter. "These jobs you do—"

"Don't, Kayla." His voice held a couched warning, but she pushed on.

"They take so much from you—I can see that. And I'm not asking you to tell me what you do. I can guess that and I'm probably right. But what I want to know is, what do these jobs do for you?"

He was taken aback by the question. His voice, when he spoke, sounded rough as it he hadn't used it so much over the past weeks. "They give me what I need."

"What I can't?" The instant the words came out, she regretted them, but she couldn't take them back.

"You shouldn't even want to try," was his answer. And still, even after that, she kissed him, cradling his face in her palms until he pushed up with a vicious groan and spread her thighs.

The next morning, she was sore and satiated. She woke wrapped around Teige, who didn't seem to mind.

"You stayed longer than you were supposed to, right?"

"Again with the psychic thing. But yes, I have to leave within the hour." He motioned toward her shower. "Mind?"

"No. I'll make you some breakfast."

"You don't know how to cook," he reminded her.

"I won't screw up eggs. Much."

He snorted and walked naked to the shower. She watched the subtle movements of his broad back until he was out of sight, and then she pulled on a long T-shirt and went downstairs. After letting Hanny out and feeding her, she started to crack the eggs.

He came down to the kitchen naked, called, "I'm going to get clothes," and walked out of the house. She supposed there wasn't anyone to see him but it still made her cover her mouth and laugh.

When he came back, he wore jeans and a T-shirt, carried a full-looking camo bag and a new bag of food for Hanny.

"I want to give you a number to call if you need me," he said suddenly. "It's not direct but—"

"I'd like that. There's a pad and paper in that drawer."

"You're the only one using pen and paper these days."

"I like them. Makes things seem more permanent." She paused. "You want to scramble the eggs while I shower?"

He snorted again and she took it as a yes. Went upstairs and washed off quickly, even though she hated losing his scent.

She'd stepped out of the shower, pulled on underwear

when he walked in. She knew instantly what he'd found in the drawer before he held the picture up.

"You shouldn't have looked through my things," she said for lack of anything better.

"Nice try. You told me to look for a pen in there," he reminded her.

Maybe she'd wanted to get caught.

"I think you owe me," he told her, and only then did she realize he had her camera in his other hand. "How about I get to take a picture of you?"

"How about if I rip your picture up instead?"

His mouth tugged a little to the left. "You've had it for a while now. Beyond that, don't you want it anymore?"

She couldn't deny it. It helped, especially when he was away.

He stared down at it, then back at her. He wasn't mad. Weeks ago, he would've been, but not now.

"Fine. One picture."

"More than one and you can pick."

"Look how that ended up." She put her hands on her hips. "One shot."

He nodded, lifted the camera. She wasn't going to smile, not until he said, "I guess we'll do it topless."

She'd forgotten completely. Crossed her arms over her bare breasts, bent down a little and laughed.

That's the shot he took.

"That's not fair."

"That's the only way I play."

He wouldn't let her see it until he'd printed it out. Only then he passed it over and she tried to study herself dispassionately. Did she realize how long it had been since she'd seen a picture of herself?

Looking into a mirror was one thing, but this was another entirely, a moment in time, never to be recreated.

She looked...happy. Pretty. Exposed, but not in a terrifying way.

In his eyes, this was how Teige saw her.

Wordlessly, she handed it back to him. He smiled, placed it carefully inside his jacket and then turned back to her.

She'd dropped her hands to her sides. Felt more comfortable naked with him than she ever had. All of this was happening so quickly and she had no safety net.

Except Teige. He looked at her like she was everything. He was, without a doubt, the strongest man she'd ever known, the most dominant.

The only one who never made her feel weak, not for wanting to hand over or lose control...not for wanting to forget.

He was the first man she wanted to tell all her secrets to. And that scared her more than anything else.

Chapter 18

TEIGE LEFT after eggs and another round of sex on the counter with her hands held over her head, following his directives. Kayla goddamned burned for him and wandered around the house in a daze for the next twenty-four hours, touching the pad with his number on it every time she passed the hallway table. She'd left his picture out too—he'd taken the one of her with him, placed it carefully inside a book in his backpack and left with that all-knowing smile that made her shiver.

An hour later, the horrible feeling she'd had days earlier was back. She was nearly doubled over, nauseous, afraid to move. When the phone rang, she knew it was Abby calling, the way she'd known Mara had a new victim. She managed to grab the phone, whisper hello before Abby said, "Kayla..."

"Just tell me," she bit out.

"There's more."

Abby paused and then told her, "Another juror's missing."

"It just happened."

"We think so."

"I thought they were all protected."

"They were. At least, they were told. Offered protection. Some of them couldn't give up their jobs, and this woman was one of them. She had to go on a business trip. She got off her plane but she never came home."

And she wouldn't. Kayla didn't have to close her eyes to picture Mara's face. More and more, she thought of her twin as an avenger, torn between protecting Kayla and killing her.

She had a feeling that these days, she was leaning more toward the latter.

Maybe it was what Kayla deserved all along. "They won't find her," she told Abby before hanging up on her. Because what else was there to say?

Besides, she wasn't able to hold in the heavy, choking sobs any longer. Her body wrenched from them and it was for the victims, for herself. And for something else she wished she'd never experienced.

Damn you, Teige, she thought, even as Hanny came closer. She'd remained on the periphery, as if guarding while Kayla had been unable to move. Now, she nosed at Kayla's face, and Kayla buried her cheek in the soft fur as Hanny whimpered for her softly, like she felt Kayla's pain.

Kayla was crying for something—someone—she never had. Teige had told her he'd had to be a bastard to survive, expecting her to not understand. But she did. It set off reminder bells in her head. She was too close. She'd already created a danger zone far more potent than any of the others.

Mara would know that, would feel it, and while Kayla had never actually forgotten that, she'd prefer to pretend that it wouldn't happen this time. In truth, she'd been so worried about Teige that she'd let herself forget everything.

Mara would find her eventually, even if it was simply by Kayla presenting herself to her sister. Kayla refused to let Teige pay the price. She refused to let that happen.

She would run. At first, she'd do it to escape the marshals and then she'd find Mara, stop the killing once and for all. It wasn't fair for people to be killed because of her. She needed to end it.

Giving up the man she might be able to love seemed the right price to pay. Because there was always a price.

She packed quickly. It was a benefit of living out of suitcases all these years—she had it down to an art form. The cameras went into a separate bag, and she hesitated, holding the picture of Teige.

To take it would be torture. It would also clue Mara in that she had someone she cared about.

In the end, she slit the lining of her suitcase and slid the picture inside. She zipped it up tight, packed the camera, left the keys behind. Hanny watched her the entire time, head tilted, and Kayla avoided looking the dog in the eyes, because Hanny knew. Whimpered when Kayla put the leash on her and got her into the front seat, then dragged her suitcases and a few other boxes into the backseat.

The rest, she'd leave behind. Nothing was that important...except Teige. And she couldn't have him. She locked the keys inside the house, gave a head tilt in Old Man Kennen's direction and then closed the door behind her.

Then she drove to Penny's house, instead of Roy's. Because Roy would alert Teige and that wouldn't give her enough time.

Penny answered the door, her hair wet from the shower. "Everything okay, hon?"

"Will you watch Hanny for me? I'll let Teige's friend know where to find her—it's just that he's not home now and I can't wait."

"Sure, as long as someone grabs her tomorrow. I got a callback for a commercial from the new headshots—I leave for New York tomorrow afternoon." Penny took the leash and Hanny went easily enough, but not without a backward glare at Kayla. Penny dug her fingers into Hanny's thick fur behind her ears. "Hey, pretty girl. You're going to keep me company tonight?"

"That's awesome about the callback. You sure it's okay with Hanny tonight?"

Penny glanced up at her. "Of course. Everything okay?"

"Speaking of jobs, I got a last minute one—assisting a

photographer for a wedding in Delaware, so I'll be gone for a couple of days," she lied.

"That's great! I guess we're bringing each other luck."

Kayla's stomach lurched. "Listen, I'll call Roy and leave him a message, but I'm sure he'll be able to grab Hanny for you in the morning."

The good thing was that Penny knew Kayla couldn't just get in touch with Teige at the drop of a hat.

Now, Hanny whined for her, like she knew it was part lie. It didn't matter—Penny wouldn't let anything happen to Hanny, and she knew Roy. It would all get straightened out.

Penny offered, "Let me give him a call. If he can't, then I'll leave him with John. I won't be in the city long."

"You know, that would be great. I really need to get on the road." She bent down to hug Hanny, whispered, "Be good, okay? Take care of him for me."

She stood, her knee cracking the way it always had since she'd fallen over a stone wall as a teen, running from the police. It cracked the same way that night when Hoss died.

She was down the walk and in the truck before either the memory or Penny could stop her. She turned the radio up as loud as she could stand it, opened the windows for the rush of air.

Bruce Springsteen serenaded her about being blinded by the light and Creedence with "Heard It Through The Grapevine." She tried to lose herself in the music so she didn't have to think.

When she did, she fought tears. Reminded herself that

she was doing the right thing, because the wrong one would've been staying put and keeping Teige, Penny, Mrs. Mueller and the rest of the town in danger. She'd move to the middle of nowhere, to a big, impersonal city where no one noticed her.

Where she wouldn't make friends who'd remind her that she wanted a life.

Chapter 19

TEIGE KNEW something was wrong when he pulled into his driveway and saw that Kayla's house was completely dark. It was nearly eleven at night and there was no fucking way she'd be sleeping in the dark.

He left his car running and knocked on her door. He gave her five seconds before went around back and broke into the old porch door. There were no signs of a break-in and once inside, no signs of a struggle. Just emptiness and the keys in an envelope for Mrs. Mueller.

And a note for him. *Hanny's safe with Penny.*

She'd left in a hurry, but she'd been concerned enough to let him know that Hanny was okay.

What the fuck was going on?

He didn't bother calling Penny, instead going right to her house and surprising her.

"I didn't think you were in town," Penny said as Hanny whimpered at his side, looking as lost as Teige suddenly felt. "Kayla tried Roy first but he wasn't answering."

Right. "I had a change of plans—she left a message but I could barely hear it."

"She said she got a last-minute job, photographing a wedding in Delaware," Penny explained. "I could keep Hanny tonight if you need me to."

"Thanks, Penny—I'm okay." He was the furthest fucking thing from it. But he couldn't tell Penny about the keys, the empty house and no forwarding address. Instead, he loaded Hanny into the car, went home and got right on the computer.

He rarely called in favors, but this time, he did so immediately. He logged into the database that his friend, Conroy, sent him the link for and found that Kayla'd only existed for about three months. Before that, nothing. Which meant she'd either made up her own identity and was some kind of grifter...or WITSEC had made it up for her. The latter made far more sense than the former.

What it didn't explain was why she'd hightailed it out of there. Something else must've happened to spook her.

His fingers went to the phone and he scrolled to Abby's name. But before he called her, he reached into his bag and pulled out Kayla's picture. He'd stuck it into the book he'd been reading so he didn't wreck it. Now, he scanned it and used the high-tech facial recognition software. It took several moments to turn her up...but he wasn't sure it was actually her.

The hair was different, but otherwise, the faces were identical.

Mara Cooper. Murderer. Fugitive. On the run.

Something was very, very wrong. A few keystrokes and the pieces started coming together, just in time for a knock at the door.

It was Abby, and she looked worried as hell.

"I was going to call you, sis," he said, then pointed to the computer.

She eyed him warily. "What do you know?"

"More than you told me, which isn't saying much."

"She's been checking in twice a day," Abby admitted.

"Ah fuck, Abs." He glanced over to the house as if magically expecting the lights to go on. "She's yours."

"I couldn't—" she started.

He held up a hand. "Don't tell me more—no reason to lose your job over something I already know." He turned the laptop's screen toward her, Mara's face on full display. In the background, there was a blurred picture of Kayla. Younger. Lighter hair. They looked exactly the same. "You hoped that somehow I'd get involved."

Abby didn't tell him anything else, just let him scan more of the story on Google. It was all there, laid out in article after sensational article.

Kayla. Aka Claire Cooper, testifying against her identical twin sister, Mara. Now dubbed a serial killer, she escaped on her first night in the psych hospital.

It was a pretty damned big secret. A reason to be afraid of the dark... especially in light of the new murders, Abby informed him.

"I know you probably don't understand," she continued.

"Ah, Christ, Abs, I do. But fuck, why blindside me with things like this? You could've—"

"Told you? Yeah, right."

"Did you think—"

"That you and she would be sleeping together?" She shrugged guiltily. "I'd hoped."

"Why's that?"

"She's perfect for you. She would understand."

"So I can't be with someone who's not being stalked by a killer? Do you realize how fucked that sounds?" he demanded. Abby nodded. But what was done was done. "Why's she running now?"

"Mara killed again and Kayla knows just before it happens. They've got that weird twin thing going on."

"So she knows and can't do a damned thing about it," Teige muttered, feeling the past weigh down on his shoulder like a brick wall. "Better she not know. But with every death..."

"She feels responsible," Abby finished. "I yelled at her the other day. She was feeling sorry for herself."

"And yelling helps that?"

"Don't give me that—the military thinks yelling's a cure for everything."

"True."

"You know that Mom would've wanted it this way."

"Mom wanted a lot of things, yes?" And she hadn't gotten any of them until goddamned now. He dragged his hands through his hair, then threaded them behind his neck as he studied his sister.

Abs had always been beautiful; incongruous in a suit

with a structured jacket and pants that all feds and detectives seemed to favor. The white button-down shirt looked crisp and perfect, even after a long day and her hair was blond and worn long and straight down her back.

She'd been exactly the Black Magic Killer's type—and he would've killed her if he'd had the time. Instead, Abby was the only victim in his history who'd gotten away.

Their father hadn't. "What do you expect me to do—chase her?" he demanded.

"Yes. Why, what do you want to do? Besides take her to bed. Again."

"She told you?"

"No, you just did."

He turned away from her and stared at the screen again. He'd always seen patterns in everything. He'd done it with teammates and townspeople because he couldn't shut it off. Thankfully, he hadn't run across a serial killer among them. Yet. There were, at any given time, fifty-plus loose in the world.

If he and Abby had gone into profiling, they'd be opening themselves up to become targets because of who their dad was. Their deaths would be trophies to the right copycat killer looking for the notoriety they would bring.

That's how his father had begun to think of the victims —trophies, not people. Probably thought that would make the job easier on him.

It hadn't. And Teige wasn't sure it ever fooled the man anyway.

"I have a DVD," Abby admitted now. She pulled it out of her pocket and handed it to Teige. He took it, flipped it between his fingers for a few moments. He knew that once he looked, there was no turning back.

Hell, there'd been no turning back from the moment he'd touched her in the rain. He put the disk into his computer and Abby moved closer, like she was trying to protect him.

The DVD opened with a shot of Mara. Her eyes, they looked dead. But with a practiced smile and a raise of her brows, she looked too much like Kayla for him to deal with. He shut it off and looked up at Abby.

She looked shaken. "It's freaky."

"Abs, listen."

"I'm involved. There's a reason. Always a reason." She paused and then admitted, "Her last handler was killed by Mara."

"Hoss? Motherfucker."

"Teige, look..."

"Don't." He held up a hand, hating the expression on her face. He didn't know if he was angrier at the fact she'd place a vic like this next to him or because she let herself get involved in a case like this.

Before the Academy, Abby had undergone rigorous psych evals. Because even though she was one of the strongest women he knew, and the testing showed that, there was no way to accurately predict how she would ever handle stress that was similar to her own.

Teige guessed he knew now.

"You always knew you'd get pulled in."

"That's your wide-eyed fantasy, Abby, not mine. I don't need to chase monsters to feel complete."

Even though his sister recoiled at his words, she didn't break down. She never had, except for that one terrible night when she'd been too terrified to do anything but shake. No one blamed her, but since she blamed herself, that was all that mattered.

"How the hell could you do this to me?" he demanded.

"I didn't do it for the reasons you think."

"What, then?"

"She seemed...right for you. She could handle you."

"That's the most ridiculous thing I've ever heard." He wanted to explode. Smash the computer. Do something...*anything*. Instead, he asked, "Is this your catharsis?"

"Maybe. God knows it scares me to death. Evil's knocking...and I'm going to open the door." She smiled wanly as she repeated their father's words. She looked ten to him, still in pigtails, holding the plastic whiffle ball bat in one hand.

"*Chip off the old block, Abs,*" Dad used to say, and he was right—she was. But she didn't want that kind of life. Couldn't.

Some people were fueled by past injustices. Abby wasn't an exception, but she was smarter, because she refused to meet the devil head-on, because she knew what she could handle.

Until now.

"Why her?" Teige demanded.

"I can't explain it any more than you," she offered, and maybe that's what bothered him the most.

He stared at the picture Google pulled up. Kayla. Hair

was shorter now and darker. Eyes were the same. The glasses she wore in an attempt to disguise them didn't do shit.

"She gets death threats," Abby added. "I don't forward them to her but they come in pretty frequently. A lot of people think she's guilty."

"And her sister's not?"

"Some say they did it together, that Mara couldn't have escaped without Kayla's help. They dressed alike during the trial on purpose, to confuse everyone. Turned the guards all around. Do you think..." Abby trailed off as she played with the coffee mug.

"Do you?"

She stared down at the folder. "Kayla lives with everyone being suspicious of her."

"With good reason?"

"I don't think so."

"Tell me why."

"Because she feels."

Teige turned to the window that faced Kayla's house. "She does."

"So we agree that she's not Mara's partner in crime."

"Agreed." He turned to her. "Where do we go from here?"

"Find her, thanks to the GPS I put on her truck when she first came to town. Then keep her safe."

Teige didn't nod...and after a moment's hesitation simply said, "Maybe we should end her nightmare instead."

"I'd love to," Abby told her brother quietly. "But that's not my department."

"Right. Not mine either, but yet somehow..." He trailed off. "Tell me about Hoss."

Hoss. He hadn't told her what kind of case he'd caught, just that he was being relocated with the witness. He seemed content. Happy, even, although she rarely saw him like that for long.

He was often a grumpy old teddy bear, which anyone who spent more than a minute with him knew.

"Were she and Hoss?" Teige asked now, the way Jacoby had weeks earlier.

She thought back to her then reaction, and to her then answer. "I don't know anything I thought I did."

"Ah, Abs, yes you do," Teige said seriously.

"I messed this up."

"No, actually you didn't. Your instincts were right on target."

"Putting her with you saved her life."

"Putting her next to me made me feel again, so you saved mine," he said bluntly and her eyes filled with tears briefly before she hastily brushed them away.

"Great," she said, all business again. "Now let's go save her for good."

"I wish it were that goddamned easy, Abs."

"Me too," she whispered as she walked out of Teige's house.

Chapter 20

THE NIGHT'S drive was the longest and loneliest she'd ever done, and she'd done plenty. Music blared to keep her head from going to the bad place, her phone turned off so she wouldn't have to see Abby and Teige's numbers pop up over and over. Or so she wouldn't have to see Teige's number not pop up.

People ran from WITSEC all the time. She wouldn't be the first. Maybe she should've done this from the start. Running from Mara had gotten her nowhere.

And where do you think confronting her's going to get you?

She shivered as the familiar chill went up her spine. "Fuck, Mara, don't. You can have me. Just let whoever you've got go."

If only it were that simple.

And maybe it was. Maybe once she settled into a motel and concentrated, she could call Mara to her. Otherwise, there was no other way—it wasn't like she had Mara's phone number.

Finally, when dawn broke on the horizon, Kayla pulled over somewhere in Georgia. The motel she found was the same as any she'd seen. Depressing. Semi-clean. She stripped the comforter off, put her own sheet down and then wrapped herself in her own blanket like a burrito. She'd catch the necessary sleep and be back on the road as soon as the dark threatened.

She charged her phone without turning it on. She missed Teige, not just because he was a warm body in bed with her. Not just because he'd try to protect her, or because he was strong.

He made her feel strong, and that was the key to everything.

She had to will herself not to cry. Tears solved nothing and they made her feel weak and unsure. She'd had enough of that to last a lifetime.

She stared at her camera on the night table, thought about what Abby told her, harsh words for a harsh truth that Kayla had needed to hear.

You can have as empty or as full of a life as you want. What exactly did you give up when you entered WITSEC? Hanging around, screwing, drinking, drugging? Whining about how you don't know what you want to be when you grow up? Yeah, I really feel bad for you that you had to give up all of that. I really do.

She wondered if she could truly have a full life the way things stood. She could still take pictures, hide behind her new name and newly dyed hair. At the moment, photography was the only thing that held her interest for any length of time (*except, of course, for Teige*, she reminded herself wryly, then told herself to shut up), but to be honest, as Abby knew, Kayla hadn't done much of anything.

She felt paper-thin, absorbed the new aliases too quickly until they drowned her. She was a shell, putting on a new mask, not in a robotic, *this will save your life* way but more of a *why does it matter because Claire Cooper was never anyone special*. She was simply notorious.

Granted, in this day and age, that seemed to be enough to get you through the door, with fame and fortune often to follow.

She put her head down and fell asleep, more stress than anything. She must've slept more heavily than she'd thought, woke to headlights shining in her window for a long moment until they cut off. She fumbled for the alarm and realized it hadn't gone off. Dammit.

A knock on the door made her freeze.

Probably just the manager. Or housekeeping.

She moved noiselessly to the door and peeked out. Her knees nearly gave way from surprise, even though they shouldn't have when she heard Teige demand calmly, "Open the door or I'll break it down to make sure you're safe."

He knew. Everything. Concern and anger mixed in his tone, and she backed away and grabbed her stuff. The bathroom had a window she could crawl out of.

"Going somewhere?"

She'd made it to the bathroom door when Teige's voice

came up from directly behind her; she panicked, went to draw her gun on him but he was too close.

He stopped her arm easily with a hand locked on her wrist. "Don't, Kayla."

"Just let me go."

"Why are you running?"

"I'm paid up on my rent. If Mrs. Mueller wants more—"

"That's not the reason I'm standing here." The cheap neon lights flashed through the window, splaying across his face.

He wasn't mad and that didn't make any sense at all. "Then why are you here?"

He wore all black tonight, and he looked predatory. In charge. His body filled the empty space, "You're coming home."

"That's not home."

"You said it felt like it to you."

"I lied."

"You're lying now." He bent his head down to whisper that last line to her.

"You know."

"Yes." He didn't tear his gaze away. "Abby's with me."

She blinked in surprise. "The marshal's got you involved?"

Now it was his turn to hesitate. He frowned a little when he said, "She's my sister."

She wasn't sure exactly how betrayed to feel about that. "Did she use petty cash to pay you to sleep with her witness or is this government-funded?"

He blinked, obviously insulted, but hell, that made two of them.

The old Claire was going to come out sooner or later—rebellious, strong, not giving a shit. Granted, she'd been going down the wrong path in life with boys and drugs and maybe she'd never been in control, but maybe that was part of the fun.

"Abby didn't tell me shit until you went missing, but I'd always suspected something. How could I not? I'm a suspicious bastard."

"If you know everything, then you should be letting me go. I'm too dangerous."

"No—you're in danger. I'll keep you safe."

"But you won't be. I won't put anyone else's life in danger."

"I signed up for it," Abby said quietly from the doorway. "I knew, Kayla."

"Claire, please. Cards on the table here. This is the end of the line. No more pretending."

"I'm not," Abby said simply, and then she walked out of the room, leaving Teige to echo, "I'm not either."

Kayla pleaded, "You can't protect me. No one can."

"I'm not just anyone, Kayla. You trust me on that."

"You lied about having a job," she said, and he didn't deny it. "You just needed to get away from me."

"I needed to get away from *me*. I thought you might be the first woman to ever understand that."

She did, dammit. She was, although she refused to admit it. "You don't owe me anything."

"You owe me—you were supposed to watch Hanny."

"I left her in good hands. I'd never let anything happen to her."

"I don't trust her to just anyone—you have to know that." He took her into his arms them, cupped a hand under her chin so she was forced to look into his eyes. "No one is getting past me, Kayla. I can promise you that."

She wanted to believe him, but she couldn't. "I can't go back."

"But I want you to come back. And you'll stay with me."

"She'll kill you. I know how she works."

"No faith in me?" He wasn't begging—that wasn't in him—but goddamned, his heart had nearly ripped from his chest when she'd gone. Having her back now, smelling the sweet fruity scent of her shampoo, seeing the scatter of freckles under her nose made him want to gather her and never let go, no matter what her wishes were. "If you don't want to come back to me—"

"I do, Teige."

"Come home."

"I don't have a home."

"You don't want one. If you did, you'd fight for it."

"And make innocents my casualties?"

"I don't see anyone innocent standing in this room." He took up all the space around her—all the air, all her desire pulled to him. "Come back with me."

"I got the last marshal killed."

"Unless you shot him, you didn't."

"Everyone thinks I'm guilty."

"Are you?"

She stared at him. "I don't know."

"Sometimes, you have to take a stand."

"I'm terrified," she admitted.

"Fear's not a bad thing in most situations," he told her. "Confidence will kill you. Fear keeps you on your toes."

She'd never thought of it like that.

"What scares you most, Kayla?"

He'd asked, point blank, his jungle-green eyes never unlocking from hers.

She swallowed, wanted to say, "Everything" but instead she told him, "You."

He nodded, cupped her face for a second and said, "Pack and stow your baggage, princess. I'm going to kiss you now."

And he did, his mouth covering hers, reminding her of why she hadn't wanted to leave him in the first place. His tongue dueled with hers, hotly demanding as her body surged with arousal. His hand cupped the back of her neck, and she ended up grabbing both his biceps—for support, and to make sure he didn't stop kissing her too soon.

She groaned into his mouth when his free hand caressed her nipple through her shirt and yes, she was done for. She would go back with him.

When he pulled back, she let him, if for no other reason than she was afraid she'd start tearing off his clothes immediately.

She blinked, hard. "I couldn't tell you before."

"I know how WITSEC works. I get it." He bent down then and he kissed her, until the resistance left her, until she knew she didn't want to live without Teige's arms around her, his mouth on hers...never wanted to forget the way he murmured her name after they'd made love.

This was a man who'd seen it all and was still willing to walk through the fire with her. Could she live with herself if something happened to him?

Could she live without him if she left? It was a no-win situation, the exact kind Mara seemed to love putting her in. And suddenly, instead of the fear, she was angry at her —furious, actually, at the way Mara had been manipulating her.

"I'll go back with you," she told him firmly. "And the next time I see Mara—"

"You won't be alone," Teige promised.

Chapter 21

ON THE RIDE BACK, Teige drove Kayla's truck with Abby escorting them along the highway. Kayla was mostly silent, and Teige figured she'd fallen asleep, until she said, "Abby told me...about your father. How he died."

Teige nodded tightly. "He was murdered by the serial killer he hunted for ten years. And he almost killed Abby too. She's a survivor."

"She told me when she was mad at me for feeling sorry for myself," Kayla practically whispered. "I deserved it."

He reached out and squeezed her thigh and she grabbed his hand. They rested elbows on the middle console, fingers entwined. "You've both been through hell. She's come out the other side."

"And now I'm bringing her back in."

"She did that to herself, Kayla."

"I'm sure you tried to talk her out of it."

"More times than I can count. And she listened, until now. She was close to Hoss," Teige told her.

"Can I...ask you about your father? That case?"

Teige nodded, his insides feeling strangely hollow at the thought. But if it helped Kayla, if it got her to talk... "What do you want to know?"

"I can't remember much of anything before my parents died in the fire when I was eight. I don't even remember the fire—I've got this giant hole in my life that Mara would fill in, but her words never jarred anything." She shook her head. "Does Abby remember everything about her attack? Do you?"

"Abby remembers everything, including the night she was attacked," he said quietly. "I wasn't there for that. I wish to hell I'd been." He paused, tightened his hands on the wheel before pushing through the memories and continuing. "I was ten when he first got on the case. The Black Magic Killer was pretty big news, but Abby and I were kept sheltered from it. And at first, the killings were pretty slow and disorganized. It wasn't until about four years into it that he organized himself and they knew they had a tried-and-true serial killer on their hands. And then, there was the cat and mouse game they began to play."

"Your dad and the killer?"

"Yes. There was contact, in the form of calls and notes. And dad started working crazy hours. He barely came home and when he did, he wasn't himself. After a certain point, it became impossible to shield me or Abby, because the killer began to threaten us, telling Dad that we were next." He heard her gasp a little. "So I remember being worried. All the time. But I'm not sure worried's the right word. More like..."

"High alert?" she suggested.

"Yeah, that's it. Can't ever turn off. You might as well be doing the hunting." He paused. "I know you're worried that you're like Mara. I've got to tell you, profilers are much closer to Mara, to being like her, than you are."

He turned to see her staring at him. "That's both comforting and horrifying."

"My father was consumed by it, so we became the same way. Practically drowned in it," he told her. "It got to the point where he didn't think of anything else, because we were never, ever safe."

"I know the feeling," she muttered as he pulled her truck into her driveway. Abby had pulled into Teige's driveway, and headed inside. Teige didn't doubt she'd sneak out the back and head into Kayla's house to clear it.

He turned and ran his knuckles along Kayla's cheek. "I know, babe—you know exactly what I'm talking about. You're consumed by Mara's life. And you want to work on security instead of other things."

"I know when she's going to kill, Teige. Do you know what that's like? Knowing and being unable to do anything about it?"

"Yeah, I can imagine. But instead of focusing on what you can't do about that, you need to focus on how you can help. You've got to put yourself back there now. Gotta think about your past."

"I've never stopped."

"You have. All you think about is surface shit. You won't let yourself remember. But if you want to save your life...if you really want to know what Mara's talking about, why she's so mad at you...you know you have to get that memory back any way you can."

He was right. She hated him for it, but if she allowed herself to go back there... "I'll drown."

"I won't let you," he said firmly, the strong hand laced in hers a symbol of that promise. "I won't let go."

"No matter what?"

"No matter what."

"It could get so ugly."

"That doesn't scare me, Kayla. The thought of doing nothing is the only thing that does."

After he spoke, his phone rang—Abby, still inside Kayla's house. He'd seen her walk across the driveway from his into Kayla's.

"Both houses are clear," she confirmed now. "I'll stay at Kayla's tonight."

"Good idea." He glanced at Kayla. "Kayla will stay with me."

"I figured as much. Send her into her house and meet her in the back." She didn't have to add, *In case we're being watched.* All of them were acutely aware of that possibility, no one more so than Kayla. She was fidgeting now, attempting to not appear nervous, which made her seem more so. "Head into your house. Abby's there—I'll meet you around back and bring you over to mine."

"And then Abby—"

"Will be doing her job," he finished.

"She's going to be in trouble," she whispered.

"I doubt it, but let's not attempt to make her job even

harder," he reasoned. At that, she nodded and got out of her car.

Chapter 22

AFTER SECRETING Kayla into Teige's, Abby left Teige and Kayla alone. It was mainly in the hopes that Teige could get Kayla to stop thinking about running.

At this point, Kayla wasn't the only one in danger. Mara had already killed one marshal to prove a point to Kayla...now Abby had herself and her brother on the firing line.

Reluctantly, she did what she'd been putting off and dialed Jacoby's number. "Did I wake you?"

Jacoby's voice was graveled but no less sarcastic when he answered, "It's four fucking a.m. and you've been MIA. Do you think I sleep when my partner and my witness are missing?"

It was fury, not sleep, keeping his voice tight and rough. Her stomach churned. She took a deep breath and said, "The diner?" because she didn't want him to meet her here.

"In ten, Abby. I'm not fucking kidding." He hung up

and she started driving, not sure if she was more angry with his attitude or her own fuck up.

I got Kayla back. Things are under control. This was my goddamned case first. All those phrases repeated themselves in her mind over and over as she attempted to justify why she ignored twenty-plus calls from him.

She was lucky he hadn't involved the state police or worse—their supervisor. But luck wasn't the first word that came to mind when she pulled into the diner's parking lot and saw Jacoby waiting for her by the front door. His stance was casual but his expression was rigid.

Shit. She got out, phone in hand and walked past him into the diner. She could feel his fury, but he'd picked a public place for them to meet, which she hoped meant he wanted to keep it together.

She picked a back booth—the diner was relatively empty—and he slid in across from her. And then he waited until both of them had ordered and the coffee had been served before saying, "Thanks for checking in. Been covering both our asses, which would've been easier to do if I'd known what the fuck was happening."

"I didn't want both of us getting in trouble," she reasoned.

He tilted his head and stared at her. "Really? That's the best you've got?"

"I'm sorry. I've been distracted. Spending too much time profiling and not enough covering this witness."

"Bullshit. You don't profile—you hate it. But you didn't mind pulling your brother into the mix." His tone was neutral, controlled, but his eyes flashed with the accusation. "Last I checked, Teige wasn't in the FBI or the marshals in any way, shape or form. Unless Lissner knows something I don't?"

"Carl knows I put Kayla next to Teige."

"Does he know you were pulling Teige into the case?"

"That wasn't my plan—"

"Does he know about last night?"

"Not unless you told him."

"Give me a goddamned reason not to, Abby," he challenged. "Because right now, I don't think you belong on this case. Probably never did."

Resisting the urge to begin with "Fuck you," she shot back, "So what, you're taking me off the case? You don't have that authority. Nothing I did made Kayla leave. You were supposed to be watching her, the same way I was. She gave no indication she'd bolt, and I got her back."

"You and your brother. Who, at the risk of sounding repetitive, last time I looked, wasn't on this case."

"With his background, his exemplary record, he's a hero. And he is again."

"Because without him, you'd never have found Kayla?" he asked.

"I tracked her from day one with a GPS."

"And if she hadn't taken her truck, you'd have been screwed." When she winced, he jabbed a finger toward her. "This kind of shit makes you look incompetent, whether you are or not. For the record, I don't think you are, but this case is way to close to your past for anyone's comfort."

She knew it. There was no way she wasn't being monitored on this one. "Who are you, Jacoby? Really? I'll drop the bullshit if you do too."

"I don't owe you shit," he muttered. He fisted his hands on the table in front of him, like he was having some kind of internal debate and finally, he murmured, "Profiler."

Profiler. Which was much different than being a US Marshal. "So you're not a marshal."

"I'm whoever I say I am—that's all you need to know."

"I won't say anything to anyone. It's just...are you with the FBI?"

"Yes. And the rest of it's a long, complicated story, and one I'm not getting into at the moment."

"So everyone else but me knows who you are—"

"Not everyone. I'm not a celebrity."

"To the FBI, you must be," she muttered almost disapprovingly, which made him grin. A little. "So they sent in a superstar to help poor little me. Because they don't think I can handle it."

"Well, you're not a profiler," he offered. "If it makes you feel any better, at this moment, you're the only one who knows what I am, okay? Not Lissner."

It did help, moderately. "But someone's been keeping an eye on me, which is why you're here. Nothing to do with who my father was, right?"

Jacoby didn't bite. "Look, I don't have time to coddle you. I told them that, but it seems like maybe they were right to worry."

"Fuck you. And whoever they are. Fuck all of you. I've done a damned good job and plan on continuing."

"That's the spirit. Cut the maudlin shit."

She took a deep breath. "Tell me this—am I expected to protect Kayla or catch Mara?"

"Can't you do both?"

"My job isn't both," she pointed out.

"Gotta aim higher, then," he told her. "For now, you do your protecting and I'll do my catch while I help you protect. Deal?"

"I'm not making deals with you."

"Hey Abby, I didn't do anything to you."

"You just hid who you are and what you're doing here."

"Could've asked."

"You wouldn't have told me straight out. Not right away. And unlike you, I don't pry."

"I didn't pry," Jacoby protested.

"But you knew my dad."

"He's a legend, Abby. Same last name, right?" he challenged.

She'd refused to change it, even after Teige changed his. "It's common."

"Not in my world," he said with a shrug. "Let's just get on with it. Both of us want to keep Kayla safe."

"I definitely do. You want to further your cover at her expense."

"Project much, Abby? Because I'm not the same guy as your dad."

"Really?"

Jacoby growled, "I don't have a family to put in danger. It's just me."

"You must have family."

Jacoby's expression tightened, telling her she'd pushed it too far. His tone was harsh when said, "I've got no one. This job necessitates that. I learned it the hard way, but the person who learned it with me was another agent. We both should've known better. I do know."

She couldn't help but say, "Sounds lonely."

"Do I want a career or love—it's my choice and I've made it. Not that lonely, but I also have more regrets than I care to talk about."

"Right. Keep it all to yourself," she said and he laughed. "What?"

There was a pause as the waitress put their plates in front of them, and then Jacoby told her, "You claim you don't want to know anything but you date a psychic."

She narrowed her eyes at him. "How the fuck do you know that?"

"Office gossip."

"Bullshit. You have no goddamned right to pry into my personal life. Ethan's entire existence is classified."

"Not to me," Jacoby said calmly.

"Asshole. And to answer your question—I don't ask him to tell me anything."

"But you could. He's your safety net."

"You can—"

"Go fuck myself. That could be the name of this investigation." He dove into his food and after a few bites, said, "For the record, I didn't want this job, didn't want to be working with someone who's as on the fence as you."

"How dare you."

"I didn't put a witness next to my brother. In hopes of what?"

"Extra protection."

"You could've refused this case."

"We both know that's not true."

He pushed his glass aside. "Spend less time worrying about me and more about your witness. She needs protecting, not me."

That's not how it seems, was on the tip of her tongue but she held back. *Do no harm, Abby.* Everyone's got their own shit to deal with. Just because you can't see through it doesn't mean it's not there. Jacoby was hiding among the marshals for reasons bigger than this case—that, Abby was sure of. "I'm staying at Kayla's tonight."

He put money on the table between them for the check. "I'll follow you back to sweep the house."

She shook her head. "I did it before and I'll do it again. I've got it under control. Have a good night, *Raz*."

He squinted at her, like he was trying to figure out what she was doing, but she just nodded and turned away.

He'd been right about one thing—keeping her witness safe was her only job.

Chapter 23

KAYLA WAS SPINNING when she got back. Overtired, the exhaustion played with her mind, and if this had been years ago she might've gone out drinking, dancing, fucking to try to forget. Relentlessly, she roamed Teige's second floor, checking windows, turning on lights, unable to focus on any one thing for too long.

Teige put a stop to that faster than she'd ever thought possible. He caught her wrist, yanked her attention to him. She looked up at him, startled, the hold on her wrist one she wasn't meant to break. But she tried, just for a second and saw the disapproval—the challenge—in his eyes.

"I don't know who I am. I'm a blank slate. The good one. Half my childhood is gone and so far, my adulthood as well. All I do is hide, stay invisible. I don't know what I want to be and what does it matter? I can't because I can't stay in one place long enough or keep one name long enough to do anything. I might as well be in prison, or dead."

"Yeah, I get that—the self-pity shit. But it doesn't suit you."

"Fuck you for thinking you know what does. You know less about me than I know about me."

"That's not true, Kayla." He circled her wrists with his fingers, mimicking the restraints he'd put on her the other night. Her face flushed, a mix of anger and embarrassment. Both because a little part of her was turning on just by this power play.

"Tell me something true about you."

"I don't want any of this. I don't want to like you. I don't mind wanting you, fucking you—but I don't want to feel a damned thing," he said.

The admission startled her. So did her anger, bubbling inside her like a volcano thundering to life. She remained still and his fingers stayed on her wrists. Could he feel her pulse racing? By the way his eyes darkened, the answer was yes. "I want to hate you."

"I know. What else do you want?" he asked. "Not that it matters. When I have my way you're only going to want what I give you."

"Teige, don't."

"Why? Can't deal with it? What can you deal with, Kayla? Or is that another secret?"

"I had to keep them."

"And now you don't. How's it feel?"

Like an avalanche. A landslide. Like she was tumbling down a hill at a hundred miles per hour and she couldn't put her hands out to stop herself. Like she was walking into a burning fire, running into a raging ocean...and she didn't care. "It feels like I want you to fuck me."

A strangled groan escaped his throat.

It was wrong to want this, especially now. There was so much, too much, going wrong. "I'm bringing you trouble," she said quickly.

He didn't argue with her. "Maybe, yes. What are you going to do about it? Bring me more?"

"I'm sure. I'm not pulling you in any further."

"You didn't. Abby did. And I can make my own goddamned decisions as to whether I'm in or out," he told her in no uncertain terms. "And I made my decisions. You don't get to tell me what to do."

"But you get to tell me."

He backed her up, pressed to her in a way that was such a turn-on. "Yeah, I do. In bed, when we're fucking. And when it comes to your safety. If you don't want to be with me? You tell me and I'll back off that part of it. But I won't back off from your safety until you are goddamned safe. Got it?" He took her other wrist, pulled her arms over her head and pushed her back to the wall. "You'll focus on me until I say otherwise."

"Teige—"

His knee forced her thighs open. "No. No backtalk."

She shuddered at the tone of his voice. His whole weight was on her. She nodded and he let go of her wrists. As soon as he did so, she wrapped her arms around his shoulders and pulled him into a kiss. A hot, hard, punishing kiss full of promises. Full of a future.

She could almost let herself believe it.

Teige's urge to tie her down and take her until she forgot everything but his own name was overwhelming. She clung to him when he kissed her, her fingertips digging into his shoulders as he carried her to the bedroom and placed her on the bed. She leaned up on her elbows and her eyes never left his as he went through his drawer, pulling out ropes.

Her eyes widened when she saw them.

Last time, he'd used her own clothes to tie her down. The rope was a bit rougher, which would stop her from fighting as much. Because even though she wanted this, he knew there was something about being tied that inspired fighting.

He stripped his shirt off and then motioned for her to lie back. She complied, albeit a little nervously. He leaned in quickly and put her arms above her head as he straddled her, catching her wrists in his hand as he roped them together, then wound the excess through his headboard.

The knots weren't tight...until she tested them. She looked at him in surprise and he smiled and said "Red to stop, yellow to slow it down. Say no all you want but I won't believe that."

She nodded, looked slightly stunned. A little relaxed, though, when he took a knife out of his back pocket and slowly cut her T-shirt open, exposing her body inch by inch. She gasped as he did the same to her bra, flicking the clasp with the shiny tip of the blade before leaning in and tugging on one of her taut nipples with his teeth and tongue.

He closed the knife, put it on the night table and pulled her jeans down roughly. His hand slid down her belly and between her legs. "Wet for me?" he asked, his voice husky, his cock heavy with longing.

"Please—yes," she managed.

"Please what? Be specific," he told her, squeezed her nipple between his thumb and forefinger, then flicked the tip with his nail. He gave her clit a quick, light touch, which made her cry out in frustration. "Just tell me."

"Please...lick me," she whispered, the blush covering her cheeks. But her eyes, now they were pure fire.

And he wasn't going to say no to her request.

God, she was beautiful. Her body surged upward to meet his every touch by his hands, his mouth. He'd tied her so there was no physical escape without the magic word, but this allowed her mind to escape the endless hamster wheel of information that only served to agitate her.

Judging by the way she writhed, escape was the furthest thing from her mind.

He tugged her jeans all the way off and buried his face between her legs, licking, sucking, laving. He'd left her legs free purposely, but when she began to roll her hips, he held them down, keeping her hostage to his tongue, his rhythm, his ways.

It didn't stop her from coming, her body alternately jerking and stiffening as the orgasm rolled through her. He didn't stop licking as she spasmed either, which made her cry out his name weakly, begging for him to *stop* and *go* and *oh Teige, more...*

Yes, there was a lot more.

———

Sated, Kayla lay against Teige's chest, hair draped across his cheek. He wanted to sleep with her against him, but he couldn't shake the feeling of impending disaster. It was both a born and bred response—he wanted her to sleep so he could sneak away and prowl.

"The cameras are working, right?" she asked.

"Guess I failed at my job of making you forget."

"Teige, you didn't fail at anything. You made me forget. That's more than anyone's ever been able to do for me."

"As long as you don't ever forget about me again, got it?" he said roughly.

She blinked. Smiled a little. "Never."

"Good." He snapped his fingers and Hanny came into the room. "Hanny will keep you company for a few minutes—I'll be quick."

He put his jeans on, leaving them unbuttoned as he walked barefoot down to the first floor. He'd slid the knife back into his pocket but that didn't matter—he had weapons hidden all around the house where he could get to them easily, if need be. Sometimes being a paranoid asshole paid off.

When he saw things were all clear on his end and in next door's yard, he texted his sister. *You all right over there?*

Not bad—talking to Ethan. I think there's a ghost here though.

He chuckled. *Old Man Kennen. Mrs. Mueller always talks about him.*

Abby answered, *I'd rather him than Mara, so I guess we're okay. How's Kayla?*

She's really good. And I plan on keeping her—and you —that way.

He waited for Abby's text to tell him that she didn't need taking care of, but instead she typed back, *Kayla's lucky. So am I.*

There was that word again.

Lucky.

Shit.

He hoped they all stayed that way...

Chapter 24

THERE WAS no time like the present, Kayla supposed. Once she was tucked into Teige's bed, wearing his T-shirt and socks, lights burning bright, she asked, "Are you sure you don't need to sleep?"

"Eventually I will. But I never have good dreams."

It was a major admission, she knew. "I wish I never dreamed," she agreed and he muttered, "Aren't we a pair?"

And they were.

In the silence that followed, Teige stroked her thighs. She realized she didn't worry about explaining the scars—he'd noticed them, but he'd never pushed her on it, never asked. Now, she told him, "I don't remember the abuse."

"So how do you know there was?"

She paused. "Mara says. And there are burns on the bottoms of my feet."

"And your inner thighs too." Her face flushed and she nodded. "I wish I didn't know what they were from. But

I'm glad you don't remember being hurt, Kayla. I can't lie about that."

"But you want me to remember the hurt."

"It's a double-edged sword. I don't think you can remember one piece of the puzzle without recalling all of it, but in this case...I think you're ready to do it. You've got me. Abby. It's time to let it all come back to you. And ultimately, safety's more important than comfort."

"To me too. I'm putting you and your sister in danger. And if that ever happened, I couldn't—"

"Don't," he said harshly. "Don't even finish that sentence, not even inside your head."

"I'm sorry."

He sighed. "My sister thinks she can make up for her childhood by taking care of other people. She hides them from the monsters."

"And you think she should be hunting them?"

"No." He said it so vehemently that she startled. "I think she's too damned close as it is. And she's not the one who should be doing penance for what happened."

"What about you?"

"I fight."

But against a different type of monster, she thought. Didn't make him any less a warrior, but as he'd already told her, it was a different kind of fight.

"I like your sister a lot," she said.

"I used to," he muttered and she couldn't help but smile. He dragged a hand through his hair. "My CO used to tell me that everything has to come full circle. I hate that he was right."

"What happened to the man who killed your father?"

"He went MIA after he left our house—he's presumed dead, mainly because there were no further kills attributed to him since. And he'd be eighty-five now so..." He shrugged. "It didn't matter. He'd accomplished what he set out to do—kill the FBI's greatest profiler to date." He swallowed. "Dad started out wanting to be the hero. The problem is that being a hero isn't a great role. It's addictive. Ego-making. I don't want to be anyone's hero."

"Too late," Kayla informed him.

It made him smile a little, before he told her, "The thing you don't get is that after this is over, you're still left with you. You have to figure out who you are, what you want. Living your life for you, not in fear." He paused. "I wanted to fight with brute force. I never wanted to fight a different kind of monster, because there's always a different one behind them. It's too personal. War isn't personal."

She didn't fully buy that, but she didn't really think Teige did either. But she thought about the other things he said, about figuring out who she was and really, she didn't know. She'd spent so much time reacting. Running. But she didn't mind Teige being rough or wild, because that was who she was—or who she'd been. She'd always had a fire inside. "I mute myself now, because the world makes me feel like I could be a killer, like Mara, because I was wild. No one believes a wild girl."

"You've got to take yourself off mute. You started to, with me."

"And look what it got me."

"That isn't because you lived the way you want to. Don't let her take anything more from you."

"I wasn't innocent. I was a punk. Drinking, fighting, screwing." She searched his face for a reaction and got none."

"So you think you deserve the life you have."

It wasn't as much a question as a statement, but she answered anyway with a shrug and told him, "Maybe I do."

"Who are you trying to bullshit—you or me?"

"You and your sister are too much alike," she muttered. "What do you want me to say?"

"I want you to give a shit."

"I've moved twelve times in the last five years. Ten during the time of the trial because of reporters who were searching me out. I couldn't go anywhere without people calling me a serial killer. Before that, I testified against my twin sister and before that, I woke up in the hospital after my biological parents were killed in a fire. So I'm sorry—how much more of a shit do you want me to give?"

"You're like the walking dead."

"Until I came here. You breathed life into me and then...look what happened. She doesn't want me to have a life."

"What were you going to do? Run away?"

She looked at him coldly. "I was going to call her to come to me. No one in law enforcement would let it happen. It was the only way it could."

"And you really think that's going to work?"

"Nothing else has, right?" She noticed he didn't argue.

"It's less about finding Mara and more about finding myself," she explained. "I realize how selfish that sounds."

"Selfish isn't always a bad thing."

"They won't let me put myself out there for Mara, so I don't know what else to do."

"You can do what I asked—talk to me about Mara. About what you're trying so hard to forget."

"I thought you didn't want to profile. I thought you wanted war."

He stared into her eyes. "Honey, if you think this isn't war…"

She pressed her lips together, a silent touché. "We're mirror twins," she explained. "Her organs are flipped. They're on the wrong side of her body. Doctors say it doesn't make a difference, but.."

She shrugged and he wondered how often she and Mara thought about the whole concept of the wrong side. It was too ironic, unsettling, almost nature's way of pinpointing exactly what was to come.

"Tell me about the twin thing—how you know Mara's going to hurt someone," Teige urged. Because now that Kayla had started talking, he wasn't about to let her stop. Not without a fight.

"It's so hard to explain. One minute, I'm reading a book and the next, I know that someone's going to die because of Mara." She paused. "It's just like that—nothing spectacular happens before a tragedy. Something should."

She looked frustrated. He understood. Sometimes, under the harsh light of day, he'd replay every moment of his worst missions, step by step, trying to figure out what the hell he could've done different. It was crucial to mission planning—the debriefing helped to ensure the same mistakes weren't made twice, but that didn't always work.

He couldn't have stopped a stray bullet from bouncing at a downward angle into Mac's skull. He couldn't make himself unlucky.

It was time to share a little more of his story to keep her from freezing up. "My CO died in front of me."

"Was it your fault?"

"No, but that doesn't stop the guilt."

"But I feel I should be able to stop Mara. I should know her well enough to do that."

Teige nodded. "I think about all the lives I could've saved."

"All the lives you have saved," Kayla corrected him. "Like you said about Abby, you know your limits."

"I do. I did. But you're pushing me past them."

"I'm sorry."

"Don't be. This is my circle. Our circle." He paused. "Hoss was Abby's instructor. Her first boss. Her mentor. That's the only reason she agreed to take you on, based on the amount of respect she had for him."

"Full circle," she echoed.

"She believes in that too." It was the truth. Abby was good with people, good with victims. She was in the right place and it had nothing to do with the fact that she was scared to be in the field. She was working her strengths. Not everyone had to chase the monsters. Not everyone could.

He knew how to find the patterns, draw the monsters out—part of it was watching his father do it relentlessly, and part of it was his innate ability to read people, to know what they were going to do next, sometimes even before they did, and to react appropriately. What he didn't know was how to chase the monsters without losing himself. He didn't think anyone did.

Kayla murmured, "I just feel...lost."

"We all get lost sometimes. Even you who can see well in the dark. Just because you can see doesn't mean you know where you're going."

"I never knew where I was going. I never fit in. This is the first place people accept me, no questions asked."

"They do have questions but they know better than to ask them," he said. "Lots of former military here, with lots of questions we can't answer."

"Your jobs were all classified."

"Pretty much."

"And the current ones?"

"Not something I'd talk about. Not something you'd want to know about."

"Because you know me so well."

"Because no one should know what I do."

"I want to know it all. I want to know everything about you, and that's never happened before," she told him honestly.

The lines around his eyes crinkled when he smiled, which wasn't often and wasn't happening now. Her gaze wandered down to his arms, his forearms roped with lean muscle, and his hands were big—the phrase "vise-like grip" was invented for those hands.

"I want to know all about you too."

"I wish I remembered more," she confessed. "I mean, I know what I was told. I know we were so poor," she said, her voice breaking a little as she recited facts she'd been forced to memorize because she couldn't remember any of it.

She figured the fact that it hurt so bad to talk about made it true.

Better you don't remember...the mind has a way of protecting you from the bad things...don't ask questions you aren't ready to know answers to.

"She was young—maybe sixteen when we were born. He was at least ten years older."

"He was your biological father."

"He's listed on the birth certificate."

Teige had his phone out and he typed something in now. Notes, no doubt, on what she was telling him. He was on a mission. He was planning.

She understood. It was the same reason she took pictures. Doing something to keep her environment in check made her feel in control.

The only time in recent memory she relished being out of control was when Teige was fucking her. She blushed hotly with those memories and in typical Teige mind-reading fashion, his eyes got heavy lidded with lust.

It was odd, going from talking about her past to feeling this way. She supposed, in an odd way, it was a good thing.

Usually, just thinking about it could put her in a funk for days.

She shifted and he put the phone down. "I'd like to avoid this too, but we need to get back to this. And then, when it's said and done and she's gone, I'm going to finally move on."

"I want that for you."

"You have no idea how badly I want to." She buried her face in her hands for a few seconds, then looked up and met his gaze steadily. "Dammit, Teige, make me."

"I'm not giving up."

She knew he referred to a lot of things, including tracking down Mara. She didn't want him to—he was already too close to danger. But telling him to stay away was as helpful as trying to get the sun to not rise.

Not going to happen.

"Give yourself some credit—look how strong you've been. You testified against her in open court."

"Every suspect has the right to face their accuser," she echoed hollowly. "It was a media circus—witness facing off against someone who looks exactly like her. She showed up looking exactly the same as I did—same dress, same hairstyle. It was like looking in a mirror. The jury was confused. Could've easily been me. In fact, I'm a little surprised she didn't try to frame me with physical evidence. I'd be sitting in jail for her crimes. If only she could find a way to match our fingerprints. First, she killed a girl from our neighborhood—the attorneys called it practice." She shuddered. "Two days later, she killed our adoptive parents. They put the crimes together after that," she explained. "She was tried as a minor, sent for a psych eval. She escaped from the locked ward—they think she had help from an orderly who went missing that same day. Haven't found any trace of her since. Mara, they've been close several times."

"But not close enough."

Kayla nodded in agreement, tugged the sleeves of her sweater down, pulled them over her hands. She was trying to disappear.

"She found you six times?"

"Twelve," she corrected. "The trial was a yearlong one. Sensationalized, because of the twin aspect."

The public had a fascination with identical twins. One was a killer—who's to say the other wasn't her accomplice? The mastermind. That's how the defense attorney tried to paint Kayla, put her on trial as the one who made Mara do her dirty work.

It was a *she said, she said* situation. And Kayla's prints were, of course, everywhere.

"It was hard for the jury to pick apart. They felt sorry for her. They started looking at me like I was the monster. Hoss told me I was still getting hate mail. Death threats. He refused to let me read them though. Abby never mentions it but I can't imagine they've suddenly stopped." She paused. "People still think I'm guilty. A lot of them think I framed Mara."

"And when she escaped, you were given a new identity and witness protection."

"New identity. I'm not sure I ever had an old one." She

laughed, almost bitterly. "All I did was try to stay out of her way."

She'd told this story countless times to countless law enforcement professionals, lawyers, psychologists...and even though Teige hadn't asked her to start at the beginning, she did.

Her first memory was of white walls and a kind woman's face above her. She screamed anyway, picking up from where she'd left off when she'd gone unconscious, according to the police reports she forced herself to read years later. She never wanted to see the pictures and Hoss had respected that.

She'd told them to never leave them with her, because one day her resolve wouldn't be strong, and she knew she'd regret that forever.

Again, Hoss had complied. He'd protected her with his life.

She and Mara had ended up going home with the kind-faced woman and her husband, living with them for the next four years. Healing, or so Kayla had thought. Mara had nothing to heal from, but she'd fooled them all.

"Do you think your adoptive parents knew anything was wrong with Mara?" Teige asked.

She figured she needed to talk about it now—if she was going to ever get the right kind of help, the combination of Teige and Abby were it. "She's a psychopath, but people liked her better growing up. Our adoptive parents liked her better."

"Psychopaths are good at that."

"I know that now." She crossed her arms. "At the time,

it fucked me up. And I was already angry and fucked up. Fighting all the time. Making out with inappropriate boys. Stealing other girls' boyfriends away. God, Diane's right to hate me."

With that, Teige let out a laugh like she'd never heard before, an honest to goodness belly laugh, and it made her smile too.

When he could speak, he wiped the tears from his eyes and said, "Maybe you and Diane can become best friends."

She snorted. "Although I do like her car. Not the red, though. I'd want it in black. Or a sleek gray."

"I'll keep that in mind."

"The upshot is that the people who are suspicious of me have a right to be. I was a crazy kid. Mean to the other girls. They always liked Mara better. She always had the friends. It doesn't make sense."

"It doesn't matter unless you're the killer. Mara committed the crimes. She's a good actress, Kayla. Did you ever think she was faking it, playing against you, a twin version of good cop, bad cop?"

How could Mara have been that cunning? More often than not, it was Mara who comforted her, brushed her hair, told her stories to get her to sleep, especially after they moved in with the new family.

"If all that love was a lie, how can I ever believe anything else is true?" she demanded. "Maybe everyone's just acting. Most of the time, so am I."

"You can't put yourself in the same category as her. You know that on some level—you know," he told her. "Cut it the fuck out, okay?"

"I'm not allowed to have a pity party?"

"You had it. Guests are going home, candles are blown out."

"I didn't get any dessert."

"I'll give you dessert, if that's what you want." His voice was thick with lust; she pictured his cock and balls, full and heavy, swaying as he walked to her.

All of that she'd put on the table and he still wanted her. She didn't understand it, but wasn't in the right mind frame to question it either.

Chapter 25

KAYLA FELT a chill go down her spine unexpectedly. The superstition said when you got a chill, it meant someone walked across your grave. But when Kayla felt a chill, she knew it was Mara, walking across another victim's grave.

Mara felt the same connection to her, she supposed. Probably got high off Kayla's fear and frustration...enjoying the killing even more because it was being done right under Kayla's nose. But Mara had been looking out for her —she'd been interrupted from setting the fire after killing Hoss, presumably, because she'd seen Kayla coming back into the house.

Hoss's body sustained forty-five stab wounds. It hadn't matched the amount Mara had given to any other victim. Kayla was always looking for patterns too but Mara often seemed to do the opposite of what anyone expected of her —the only constant was that each killing brought Kayla more suffering.

The implication appeared to be that, if Kayla hadn't

testified against her, Mara wouldn't have committed these murders...because she wouldn't have been convicted.

But serial killers didn't simply stop. Mara would've found other reasons to kill. At least that's what the research on serial killers had proven time and time again.

After Hoss's murder, Kayla forced herself to look at those pictures, to see how much fury was behind her sister's motives. The police hadn't allowed her back inside the house to see him. And she'd only been gone ten minutes or less, as she'd been in the garage where Hoss had helped her set up a makeshift darkroom.

There was a monitor there, next to Hoss. Which meant that Mara had watched her while she'd killed Hoss.

God, she had to stop thinking about this.

Teige said you need to do the exact opposite. She had to respect the man, since he lived with nightmares of his own.

"Abby just called—a quiet night. She's headed to the office. You'll stay with me and I'll keep an eye on the house," Teige told her now. She was at the top of the stairs and he was at the door, talking to the mailman. "Hey, I'm taking in Kayla's mail for the next couple of days."

"Here you go, Teige." The mailman was the same man, rain or shine, and since it was a small town, he didn't need Teige to fill out a form or prove what he was saying was true. It was both rattling and comforting.

When he'd closed the door, she'd come down the stairs to find him looking through the mail—mostly catalogues and stuff that Abby had signed her up for in order to give the appearance that Kayla had existed before several months ago—and frowning at one of the envelopes before looking up at her.

"What's that?" she asked.

He held it up. "It's from Penny."

She took the plain white envelope from him and turned it over in her hands. "Maybe it's a check? I told her she didn't have to pay me but...maybe she got the job."

"Job?"

"She was flying to New York for a callback. Probably right after you took Hanny back from her." She tore the envelope open and stared at the picture. It took what felt like minutes for her mind to adjust to what she was seeing in front of her. Teige was behind her, his hands on her shoulders, soft at first and then the grip got tighter when he realized what—who—he was looking at.

A picture of her and Penny. Except it wasn't her with Penny. It was Mara, with Penny in New York City. The picture began to shake—she was holding it tightly, unable to let it go, trembling with fear and rage and anger.

What did this *mean*?

She couldn't put voice to those words, even though, inside her mind she was screaming it, over and over.

Penny was dead.

Finally, she heard herself screaming out loud, wanted desperately to let go of the picture but she couldn't drop it from her fingers, no matter how hard she tried.

When she finally was able to let go, there was dried, flaking blood on her hands.

Penny's blood.

She began screaming even louder.

Teige saw the blood, the picture and was dialing the phone even as he pulled her close. "Abby, get over here and bring a forensic team. And call a doctor."

She was holding her hands up to him, trying to pull away, no doubt to wash the blood off. But she couldn't, not until Abby or the police tested the blood.

The door swung open. Teige turned, relieved, but instead of Abby, it was Diane, with several police officers trailing behind her. What the... "What's wrong, Diane?"

Hanny was barking, refusing to leave Abby's side except for a brief lunge at Diane. Teige grabbed Hanny's collar and ordered her back.

"I know what she is," Diane said furiously, pointing at Kayla, moving toward them. Teige let go of Kayla to catch and drag Diane backward.

For a long second, no one said anything. As Diane struggled, Kayla took several steps toward Diane and even though Teige tried to block them from each other, Kayla got close enough to Diane to ask in a hoarse voice, "Tell me what you think I am."

"You're a killer," Diane spat.

Kayla reached out to lunge for Diane's neck, demanding, "Who told you that?"

"Your sister," Diane screeched before Teige managed to stop Kayla's hand from reaching its target. At that point, all hell broke loose. The cop tried to grab Kayla, who fought, just as Abby and Jacoby walked in. Teige managed to move Diane into the kitchen and away from everything, but somehow, Kayla wrangled loose and followed.

"You need to let the police arrest her," Diane was telling him.

"Not the time, Diane," he warned.

"It's exactly the time. She's a killer." Diane's eyes blazed judgment that branded Kayla's skin as effectively as a hot poker. "Penny's dead because of her."

"She's going to kill you," Kayla told Diane steadily.

"Are you threatening me?"

Kayla couldn't help it—she laughed at the absurdity of it. "You'll know when I am. Right now, I'm trying to save your life."

"Mara said that's what you'd say." Diane looked strangely satisfied, then she pointed at Kayla while staring hard at Teige. "You've been fucking a killer."

Teige took a step toward Diane, took her shoulders and shook her a little. "You're going to get yourself killed."

"I want Kayla arrested. There's proof she killed Penny!" Diane screamed at him.

"Circumstantial at best," Jacoby said firmly. "She'll be under surveillance. As will you."

"Don't do anything stupid, Diane," Teige warned her.

"Don't worry—I don't fuck killers."

Teige stared at her, then told her, "Yeah, you have, babe. For a long time now."

Diane just stared at him, her mouth opened in a silent O.

"Not another fucking word," he continued for good measure, his tone vicious. Even though Diane had put herself in major danger, at the moment, she wasn't his main concern. At that point, Teige told Kayla, "Stay here." And then he picked Diane up and carried her out to the porch.

Diane fought him tooth and nail. "Put me down, dammit." And when he complied, still holding her wrist so she couldn't go back in and talk to Kayla, she said, "You need to believe me."

"Then tell me the exact conversation."

Diane spoke rapidly. "She told me all about Kayla—how she's Claire. She made me go to the computer and Google the case. She waited. She let me ask questions. At the time I didn't know she had Penny. And then I told Mara that I believed her...that Claire had attacked me. And then Mara explained that she'd told Penny everything Kayla did. That Penny said she didn't know anything, that she didn't believe." She swallowed hard. "She asked me if I believed her and I told her I did. That's when I heard Penny screaming and then it was so quiet. She said she let me listen because I believed. That I could stay alive because I understood. And then she told me to go confront Claire."

"Jesus Christ." Because Diane hated Kayla, her life might end up being spared. A vicious irony, at best. "Did you give Mara Kayla's address?"

Diane shook her head. "No. She didn't ask. I was pretty damned freaked out so I wasn't speaking much."

Teige wanted to believe her, but in the end it didn't matter much either way. Mara knew where Kayla lived—she could've easily shown up there instead of simply mailing a letter. But before Teige could question Diane further, Jacoby came out onto the back porch, his eyes directed toward Diane. "Want to tell me what the fuck you're doing bringing a cop here?"

"Because Kayla's a killer. Because I heard Penny being killed." Diane wrung her hands together. Her eyes were swollen and she wore a wild, scared look he'd never seen before on her face.

"You heard Penny being killed by Kayla?"

"By Mara. Penny's dead. I know she is."

"It'd be convenient if she told you where to find the body," Jacoby commented in a completely serious tone. Diane moved to slap him, her patented move, but Jacoby was faster, grabbing her wrist, obviously used to women trying to slap him. "I want you to calm the fuck down and give me a statement. Every goddamned thing you remember." He glanced at the officer. "Tape this."

"There's a message on machine too," she said dully.

"Keys," he said, and Diane handed him the ring she'd been holding. He pointed to a plainclothes who'd just walked into the house. "Get me the machine."

The plainclothes nodded, caught the keys Jacoby threw at him and left without question.

"Kayla, don't listen to Diane," Abby was telling her.

Kayla shrugged. "She's just saying what everyone feels."

"Not everyone."

"Do you think the news will find out soon?"

"Jacoby will find out who Diane told. We'll control the press since it's an active investigation. That means Diane goes into protection and the cops shut their mouths," Abby promised, just as the doctor she'd brought along came in with a shot.

"It's for your voice," he said. "It won't knock you out."

Kayla allowed the shot, since she'd nearly screamed her voice away. When she tried to speak, it was scratchy, raw and painful-sounding. She'd screamed so loudly he wouldn't be surprised if she'd damaged her voice permanently. The doctor had confirmed as much when she'd asked him earlier, but it was the least of her worries.

And then one of the police detectives came in, that bloody picture bagged and in his hands. Before he could say anything, Abby asked her, "Kayla, are you sure this isn't you in the picture?"

Kayla shook her head hard. "It's not me. I know it's hard for everyone to understand, but even though we might look identical, I can separate me and Mara in pictures."

Abby blew out a hard breath then showed her badge to the detective. "That's her statement. I'm the marshal in charge of her case. Kayla was in my care during the time of the murder. She didn't leave the state."

"The picture shows otherwise," the detective pointed out.

Kayla couldn't help but think that she had left the state...that she'd been away from Abby and Teige for long enough to commit a murder. And depending on where

Penny's body was discovered, Abby had just perjured herself for Kayla. But all Kayla said in a hollow tone was, "The fingerprints on the envelope won't match mine. The fingerprints at the crime scene won't match mine. They never do."

It was always her only out. But Mara was getting better and better.

"Still, we have to ask questions." The detective put down a plastic bag in front of her. Inside were pieces of a picture—it was of Penny, ripped up, her eyes blacked out by a pen. "We found this inside your house in your desk— we were given permission to search it by Agent Daniels."

Abby nodded, but clenched her fists at the look of devastation on Kayla's face.

"I didn't mean...I was angry. Not at her—she was my first friend here. I called you and you yelled at me and..." She stared at Abby for a second then put her face into her palms. When she spoke again, it was muffled. "You can't believe I did this. I wasn't here."

"She was driving in the opposite direction," Abby confirmed. "There was no way she could've committed the murder."

"But she could've asked her sister to do it for her. Isn't that what you're accused of, Kayla?"

"Never proven. Because it's not true," she protested, allowing the fire to come back into her. Anything was better than feeling defeated, which she refused to be. She was innocent and Abby and Teige believed her.

"She's under my protection."

"This is an open investigation..."

"Her protected status trumps that," Abby said evenly. "I'll make sure she's available for questioning by the FBI since this is their case."

The detective scowled. "This is my town. I won't be cut off from this investigation," he warned, but he did leave the room, taking the evidence with him.

"Please hand the evidence to my colleague on your way out," Abby called. She turned back to Kayla, handed her some tissues and forced her to sit. She had her drink some more of the honeyed tea, then asked point-blank, "Was Hoss in love with you?"

"No more beating around the bush, Marshal Daniels?"

"No," Abby agreed.

"I think so. Yes. We were close, at first. He didn't try anything but if I'd made a move…"

"He would've welcomed it," Abby finished.

"At first, yes. But I wasn't ready. And when I was, well, he seemed disinterested by that point. I thought it was odd but…" Kayla's eyes went wide. "Mara. Do you think Mara…"

"It's the only way I can think of. Either Mara pretended to be you that last night…or she somehow convinced him of her innocence."

"And my guilt," Kayla muttered. "You think they were talking? That they planned to meet?"

"I think she killed Hoss to send you the message that she can get to you at every turn."

"So why didn't she? Get to me, I mean," Kayla clarified. "I'm still breathing. She could've come right to me. She could've been waiting when I found Hoss. It would've been over in seconds. Unless it's true, what Jacoby said, that Mara gets more pleasure from me being alive and 'paying' for my supposed crimes than she ever would killing me. Either way, how does she keep finding me? Tracking me? Is she having an affair with you?"

Abby smiled a little. "Not my thing. And I'm not sure she could fool me. But maybe we should have some kind of code when we see each other. That way, if I do run across Mara, I'll know the difference."

Kayla nodded. "It's the eyes, Abby. The eyes will give Mara away every single time."

"I'll remember that." Abby touched her shoulder. "What else can I do for you now?"

"I just feel helpless. Will I ever not feel that way?" Kayla practically demanded.

"It takes work. And you'll never let it go completely, but you'll have hours, and then days where you don't think about it at all," Abby told her firmly.

Kayla nodded. "You've been through hell. I'm sorry—"

"Don't be. This is my job—I chose it. No one forced it on me."

"Teige said you felt it was your destiny."

"It's as close as I could get to monsters without drowning in them." Abby brushed some hair from Kayla's face, then brought the mug up to her lips. When Kayla went to protest that she could do it herself, she realized just how badly her hands shook.

She'd heard Abby refuse the pain meds on her behalf, probably because Teige told her how much she hated them. "Thanks," and then, "I'm sorry about your father."

"It was a horrible way to die," Abby said hoarsely. "It was also horrible the way my father lived. Hunting monsters. Getting in their heads. How do you not become one."

"Was he?" Kayla asked.

"In the end, I think so. He was breaking down. Drinking. He didn't abuse us—not consciously, anyway. But he talked about that case with us."

"My God, Abby."

"He thought we should've been able to handle it. We were sixteen and seventeen when he told us everything about this guy. I think he was trying to keep us safe, like he knew he'd come after us."

And he had. She and Abby and Teige had so much more in common than she ever could've thought.

For several long moments, Teige and Jacoby stood there side by side, staring into the mess of woods behind the house.

Finally, Jacoby narrowed his eyes and turned to Teige. "Tell me about Diane."

"What about her?"

"The nature of your relationship."

"Fucking," Teige offered bluntly.

"On your end or hers?"

Teige sighed. "Both. She's possessive, but she doesn't

want a relationship. Just doesn't want me with anyone else."

"Classic," Jacoby muttered. "She jealous enough to frame Kayla?"

"Yes," Teige said firmly but then added, "Is she smart enough? Yes. But this kind of thing? Not her speed at all."

"They got into a physical fight," Jacoby reminded him.

"Kayla punched her first," Teige pointed out. "Listen, Diane isn't going to murder someone to frame Kayla. Why Diane's return address was on the envelope, I have no idea."

"Her prints were on it too," Jacoby told him. Teige just shook his head. "Do you think Diane really spoke with Mara?"

"Yeah, I do."

"Because you can tell when she's lying?"

"With Diane, almost every time she opens her mouth, she's lying," Teige said bluntly.

"Fucking shouldn't be that complicated."

"You haven't been laid in a long time or what?"

Jacoby snorted. "Touché, man." After a pause, he added, "No sign of Penny. Boyfriend's flipped out."

Teige winced. John was a good guy—a good soldier. He'd heard that name bandied around as a candidate for Delta Force. If he went in after this incident, Teige had no doubt he'd be a machine. And he didn't know if that was good or bad...for John and for the teams. Anger, channeled correctly, could be an amazing tool or a detriment. "What about Kayla?"

"She stays here." Jacoby checked his phone. "Diane's

already back home. It's being searched, phone lines checked and tapped. She's not leaving the premises. We don't need her shooting her mouth off about a killing."

Teige agreed. Mara was getting closer. If they wanted Mara to come into town, they couldn't make it more difficult for her. "So who the fuck are you?"

"I'm a US Marshal," Jacoby answered calmly.

Teige didn't bother to push it. He got undercover. Stealth. But still, "Don't fuck my sister over, because then we'll have a problem."

Jacoby nodded. In silent agreement, they went inside to find the FBI had escaped the confines of the kitchen and were milling around the hallway, with two of them in deep discussion. When they saw Jacoby and Teige, one of them said, "The FBI will stay on point with the marshals for Kayla. Plainclothes will patrol the surrounding streets."

Jacoby shook his head. "You'll stick out like sore thumbs. Trust me, there's no good way to have any of you here."

The agent glared, but Teige noticed he didn't argue. Jacoby definitely had some power. Either he was older than he appeared or he was some kind of wunderkind.

The harder Teige looked, the more haunted Jacoby seemed.

Haunted and hunting killers went hand in hand. He wanted to tell Jacoby to get out now, before it got worse, to walk away from all this and never look back.

But then Abby and Kayla would be left hanging and that's why Jacoby stayed. That's why Teige's dad had stayed, because there was always someone to save. And

Teige was sure they both promised themselves *this is the last time*...every single time.

"We can handle this," Jacoby said.

Teige didn't ask who the *we* was.

"I want to tell her to come to me." Kayla's words, spoken from where she stood in the back room's doorway. She'd snuck up on both of them, which wasn't easy to do.

"Forget it," Teige told her. Kayla ignored him, probably seeing the look of possibility on Jacoby's face. Teige narrowed his eyes as she approached them.

"Jacoby, you and I and Teige all know it's the best way. The only way."

"The best way to get yourself killed," Teige broke in. "I won't allow it."

"Won't allow it?" Kayla repeated with a fire in her eyes that made Teige hot in so many ways. "I need to do this. Otherwise, I'll never be free."

Teige hadn't asked her how she'd feel if he killed Mara...because that was his plan. "You'll kill her, Kayla? Because that's exactly what you'd need to do before she gets the upper hand. No hesitating. And I know how much guilt you feel."

She tensed at Teige's words.

Teige got closer. "You're not ready. I never want you to have to be ready for that."

"But I can defend myself. You said I need to know self-defense," she practically whispered.

"That's so different, babe. A whole different world."

Jacoby broke in. "Kayla, I'll let you do whatever you feel you need to. But Teige's right. Self-defense is nothing like lying in wait, knowing you're going to kill. It's what separates you from her. I hope you find that comforting."

"She's the only family I have. The only link to my memories," Kayla told him. "Do you know how sick it makes me feel to say that? To think, I hope she doesn't die so I can see her again? Crazy, right?"

Jacoby gave a quick shake of his head. "Not really. She wants the same exact thing. Doesn't mean she won't make it hurt like hell, though."

Chapter 26

JACOBY PAGED THROUGH A SMALL NOTEBOOK. "There are now ten murders attached to Mara, including her adoptive parents, that we know of. And if we find Penny..." He shook his head.

"Right." For every murder you see, there are two more you don't—that was her father's theory. It didn't always pan out, mainly because there were always undiscovered bodies, and most serial killers either over-bragged and over-estimated themselves or they played it close to the vest so they'd continue having people interested in them. That's what serial killers wanted—attention. Lots of it. If they couldn't keep killing, then they'd find a way to relive their kills. And they weren't about to be either humble or gracious. "I can't imagine...to have your own family wanting to do you harm. It's one thing if it's a total stranger, but family's so much harder..."

"You won't get an argument from me," Jacoby agreed, but didn't offer any more. Neither did she. Most agents—

and marshals—had fucked up pasts. It was why she'd fit in, felt comfortable despite what she'd been through. Despite her limitations.

But the one thing she did know was that Jacoby might be new to her, but he wasn't new to any of this. However unassuming and understated he acted, he knew the score. And he knew this case like the back of his hand. And he knew about Abby's past as well as Kayla's.

And we're both haunted by the ghosts of our pasts...

The only problem was, Mara wasn't a ghost. And Abby had to stop putting herself in Kayla's place. She needed to rebrand herself as a protector. Because she'd fought like hell for this job, convinced her sup that she could do it. And dammit, she would.

For Hoss. Because her father had mentored Hoss, despite their difference in agencies and positions. Hoss was her father's go-to guy when he had witnesses who needed protection from the monsters, and Hoss always came though. It became the link in the chain that held Abby, who wanted a career in law enforcement and her father, FBI legend Ryan Daniels, together with Hoss.

And while Abby had wanted law enforcement, she'd also known her limits. She knew what made her feel safe in the beginning and what didn't. But even when the Black Magic Killer disappeared, she couldn't stop looking over her shoulder.

She was as much in WITSEC as Kayla. Because at one point, Abby had been Kayla, protected by Hoss.

"You've got to stop beating yourself up," Jacoby told

her sharply. "Talk to someone about it—get it out and let it go."

"Right, sure," she said absently. "And who do you turn to?"

Jacoby pressed his lips into a grim line. "I've been taking care of myself for a long time."

Abby cleared her throat. "Yeah, me too. I don't think it's working very well for either of us."

Jacoby surprised her then by laughing, a deep belly laugh, and she joined him. Soon they were both wiping their eyes.

"We're pathetic," she managed through laughter.

"Totally," Jacoby agreed. Just then, both their phones beeped, almost in unison. They both cursed under their breaths, because that was never good.

"From Diane's house," Jacoby said. "Let's go."

They got into Abby's car, Jacoby behind the wheel as Abby dialed Teige. "Come on, pick the hell up," she muttered into the phone. When she got his voice mail, she cursed loudly, hung up and texted him several times. "No response."

"Doesn't mean anything. They're probably busy," Jacoby said.

Abby stared at the message again. *Activity at Diane's house.* That could mean anything. "She's dead, isn't she?"

"No fucking clue. That bitch could just want our attention," Jacoby muttered. "Or Teige's."

When they got there, everything seemed calm. The police officer stationed outside the door ambled up to them with an easy nod. "Everything okay?"

"We got a call that there was activity here," Jacoby said, and the officer frowned. He immediately radioed inside and got the other officers to radio back. "Stay here," he told Abby. "I'll go check."

Abby nodded, said to the officer, "No strange cars going by? No phone calls?"

"No ma'am. It's been radio silence, and I've got the calls forwarded to my number. Diane wouldn't hear them coming into the house. We figured it was better that way, mainly because she's sedated."

Abby frowned. "Did the doctor come by?"

The officer looked disturbed. "No. She was agitated for a while, walking around the back patio. We finally got her inside. Before we could stop her, she'd taken a couple of Ativans to calm down. But she's easier to deal with asleep."

"Most women are," she deadpanned and he nodded in agreement for a second before realizing he maybe shouldn't have taken that as truth and adding, "No comment."

"I'll put in for the office to trace where the hell that message came from—maybe they can pinpoint if someone's bouncing signals," Jacoby said. "Unless it's Diane, doing it in her drugged state. I'll check her phone."

"Good—you do that and I'm going to look around back," Abby told him, and when Jacoby hesitated, she waved him inside the house and began to march herself away. He obviously relented, because she heard the door close as she reached the side of the house.

Diane's backyard was mainly concrete patio that extended almost to the wooded section behind her. Abby surveyed the area but everything appeared to be in order—although it was so quiet it made the hair on her arms stand on end.

There was something wrong in her life when quiet was a bad thing.

She took a step down off the concrete patio onto the grass and that's when she noted the paper on the lawn. It was half hidden by the flagstone stepping stones that led ostensibly to the woods, framed by flowers and maybe extended twenty feet.

She glanced down and saw the page of a book, ripped out—a page she recognized immediately. "Goddammit," she muttered, because she'd almost yelled, and no, she wouldn't give anyone the satisfaction of that.

It was a picture of the crime scene at her childhood home—a picture of her father's body, unauthorized and grainy, a tabloid shot that had been shown over and over. They'd never discovered who'd taken it or sold it.

Abby grabbed the paper up and shoved it into her jacket pocket, even as she spotted another page. That one held part of her story from that night, culled from interviews with the press and hospital employees. The next one, a few feet away, at the edge of the woods, was a picture of her, again, grainy, but Abby knew she'd been covered in blood and soot, on the verge of unconsciousness and hysteria at once.

Her hand shook as she picked up the page, shoved it in her pocket with the others and took a few steps into the woods.

"Who the fuck did this?" she asked, her voice shaking

with anger.

Of course, no one answered. She walked back toward the house and went inside—Jacoby was talking with one of the officers and Abby wandered around the house, looking for a bookshelf. She found one in the small den—the only books seemed to be about Teige...and that one fucking unauthorized biography of the Black Magic Killer. She pulled it off the shelf and paged through.

The pages she'd found had been ripped out of this book.

Diane knew the family history—and Diane had always hated her. Abby recalled that every time they'd been in the same place, which Abby made sure didn't happen often, Diane would attempt to grill her about what happened that night with the Black Magic Killer. After the second time, Abby told her in no uncertain terms to never bring it up again. So Abby could definitely see the bitch doing something like this, for either Abby or maybe even Teige to find.

If the bitch was awake, she'd have dealt with it now, but there'd be time for that later.

"Hey." Jacoby came into the den as she shelved the book. "Everything okay?"

"Fine," she lied, not wanting to have to relive her past, or be asked if she was going to be okay, or if this case was too personal *again*. "How's Diane?"

"The text came from her phone. She's pretty out of it—doesn't remember texting but she's slurring and not making much sense. Maybe she was dreaming."

"Do you think Mara could've come in and out without

anyone noticing?"

"Anything's possible, but to what end?" Jacoby asked.

"To prove she can."

———

After canvassing the house and property thoroughly and finding nothing amiss, Abby and Jacoby reasoned that it was most likely a false alarm from Diane. But they both kept the other possibility in the forefront of their minds as they headed to the diner, and, at a corner booth, went over the old files on Mara and Kayla for the umpteenth time. Abby focused on the pictures from CPS from their visit with Mara and Kayla's biological parents, taken two weeks before the double-wide burned to the ground.

The pictures from their home showed the absolute squalor in which Mara and Kayla grew up. Kayla might've blocked it all out just for that alone. "They should never have been allowed to stay in this place with their parents," she murmured.

"They moved around too much. CPS would start to get a handle on them, because they noted what they believed to be possible abuse, although they never got as far as getting the girls to the doctors. They would get the hell out of Dodge when the authorities came sniffing around. The father was a drunk—he didn't work, just collected disability. He never married the mom, so she continued to collect welfare—reports have her drunk a lot of the time too, but the neighbors tended to mind their own business. He probably threatened them," Jacoby surmised.

"So what did he spend money on, then? Certainly wasn't his kids," Abby said angrily.

"Gambling, prostitutes, who knows? There were reports the wife drank. Mara maintains she was molested by her adoptive parents," Jacoby said slowly, with a pained look on his face. "She kept saying Kayla was a murderer too."

Abby didn't want to explore the possibilities of that... why Kayla didn't remember. She rubbed her palms to her forehead in an attempt to stave off the inevitable, stabbing headache. "I hate this."

Jacoby gave her a sympathetic smile. "When you're profiling, you always find out things you wish you didn't know."

She recalled her dad saying the same thing, many, *many* times over. "Jacoby?"

"Yeah"

"Do you believe in curses?"

He stared at her. "Are you trying to put one on me?"

"No. Well, maybe a little in the beginning." They both smiled at that, first ones in a while for both, but that only lasted a while because she added, "My family's cursed. I think I believe—I have to, because I've got the evidence right in front of me."

Jacoby considered that. "I believe."

"We have it the worst. Because the dead are dead. It's the survivors who are really, truly cursed. No one knows that or thinks about it. We're the brave, strong positive ones. But we're also the cursed ones. Goes hand in hand."

She noticed that Jacoby didn't disagree with her.

Chapter 27

TO KAYLA, the morning's events had been like a nightmare, something she still couldn't really believe happened.

It became more real later that afternoon when the police found Penny's body dumped under an overpass on a highway just outside of Georgia.

Georgia. And close to where Kayla—and Abby and Teige—had been. Penny had been near them when she was dying. Which meant...Mara had been so close to them too.

A sinking stone of dread tore through Kayla as she thought about how Penny must've suffered, how she must've thought Kayla had been the one to hurt her, or at least set her up. How Mara took Penny from New York to Georgia, possibly terrorizing her for the entire ride.

It should've been me. But for Mara, this was better—it was her way of ensuring Kayla suffered enough. For what crimes, Kayla still didn't know.

"What're you thinking about?" Teige asked, brows raised.

"She can't die until the job's done. Until I remember." Kayla held a hand to her throat. "If I never do..."

Teige couldn't stand to hear the pain in her voice. He put his arms around her and she rested her head against his chest as she stared out the window to the woods below.

"She'll come for me if I tell her to."

"Kayla—"

"Maybe she'll tell me."

"And then kill you."

"Diane's next," Kayla said in a quietly strangled voice.

"I'm glad you had the good sense not to say that out loud when the police were here," Teige growled.

Kayla nodded mechanically. She wasn't truly processing anything he said. Whether she was feeling Mara's intentions or it was the next logical train of thought, it didn't matter. Teige knew she was right. So did Abby, Jacoby and the FBI team who showed up at Abby's office, at Kayla's house and who were currently demanding an audience with Kayla.

And in the state she was in, Kayla would most definitely repeat, "Diane's next," to them. Which was why Abby and Jacoby agreed to keep them at bay. Teige's house was set up to the nines with perimeter alarms. He'd thought about explosives but there were too many factors involved that could become problematic. Hanny was a better perimeter alarm than anyone, which was why Teige was taking her out on a leash and bringing her right back in and putting her upstairs with Kayla. He wasn't going to let

anyone fuck with them, and Hanny would be a target for
Mara, in order to break in without being seen or heard. So
those two needed to be connected at the hip. Even though
he could tell Hanny missed her runs with him, she was also
on high alert. She knew something was up and she kept
strolling to the window to check on things.

"Where is she?"

"Diane? She's in protective custody. Or she will be."
Right now, she was no doubt surrounded by marshals and
FBI and police, telling her story over and over again,
getting more dramatic with each telling.

She's next.

Teige hoped the marshals placed Diane far enough
away so as not to draw Mara here to prove something.
They'd kept it quiet as to who killed Penny—that was their
only hope. So while the town remained in mourning, they
didn't realize there might be a killer among them who
looked like someone now considered one of their own.

Teige was getting pulled in by Kayla, by his past. He'd
fought like hell to extricate himself from it, but the net held
him fast.

He woke up with a hard start on the couch, Kayla
curled next to him, both of them having dropped off from
sheer exhaustion. The house was quiet, the TV flickered.
Hanny was calm, the most reassuring sign there was. He
trusted her more than any security camera.

Still, he patrolled the house quietly, and when he

returned, Kayla was waking up, blanket pulled around her, Hanny in front of her.

"You okay?"

"None of the detectives believed me," she said quietly.

"I did. So do Jacoby and Abby. That needs to count."

"It does," she insisted. But the night of her adoptive parents' murders kept playing over and over on a continuous loop in her head. She'd been gone overnight, partying and sleeping with her boyfriend of the moment, and she'd come home to police tape and a frantic detective. Her adoptive parents were dead and Mara had been arrested.

Kayla remembered the questioning, even though her lawyer told her later that Mara's prints were found on the weapon and she'd been covered in blood. She tried to say she'd been performing CPR but no one bought that.

Kayla had witnesses—guys she'd been partying with, and that made her look horrible. And Mara was trying to get her to lie.

In Mara's eyes, Kayla had betrayed her.

Forget the 'through Mara's eyes' part—you feel that way too. And guilt's not a good look on you.

"Are you going to keep beating yourself up over this?" Teige asked, yanking her out of her reverie.

"Penny's dead because of me, so fuck you, Teige."

"Get over this, *Claire*. Stop the pity party. Mara's a master manipulator and you're letting her control you and your life."

"I told you I wanted that to stop. I want her to come for me," she protested.

"You want her to kill you."

"That's not true."

"Bullshit. You think it'll be over, and so much easier to let her do what she wants to do."

"You don't know anything about it. You weren't the hunted one."

"But Abby was, and you've told her she doesn't understand either. The problem is, she understands all too well, and so do I. You can't get away with your shit anymore, and that scares you. And it should. But once you let it go, you'll be stronger. And, in turn, freer."

She wanted to believe him, had been chained to Mara and her crimes for so long it seemed impossible to break the bonds. "I could be a killer."

He stared at her. "Kill anyone in recent memory?"

"No. But just because I say no doesn't mean it's true? Why should you believe me? Not all that long ago, I was almost charged with Mara's crimes. I look at the evidence and I can understand why people don't always believe me."

He tilted his head to examine her. "What do you want me to say? That I think you were a cold-blooded murderer before the age of eight? Do you expect me to walk away?"

"I was ready to run. From Hoss." She whispered it, even though they were alone. "The police found my packed bag. The marshals weren't happy. A lot of them said it threw suspicion on me."

"So why were you going to run?"

"Because the walls were closing in. I felt her. And I figured, if I could make her chase me..." She shook her head. "I should've warned Hoss. But I didn't want to believe it myself for a while. And then I thought I'd been too late. Turns out, I was right."

"Why do you want me to believe you're a killer?"

"I don't," she protested. "Everyone just does."

"I'm not everyone," he growled. "So if you have anything to admit to me..."

"I don't remember anything from before my eighth birthday."

"So when does your memory start?"

"It's spotty. I remember waking up in the hospital. I thought I was dreaming about this pretty woman who always seemed to be there whenever I'd gather up strength to open my eyes. She and her husband were the ones who'd been chosen to foster us. They started the adoption process almost immediately. Turns out, she was a twin who'd lost her sister when she was younger, and she refused to separate us." Kayla gave a sound like a cross between a sob and a laugh. "I wish she had. Maybe things would've been different."

"Or maybe Mara could've framed you more efficiently," Teige reasoned and she winced. "Abby showed me the evidence. It was pretty obvious what she'd tried to do."

"She was young. She's gotten much better, much more sophisticated," Kayla told him, mimicking the FBI language she'd heard far too many times. "They also told me there are very few true female serial killers."

Teige shook his head. "I never believed that. I think women are just better at covering their tracks."

"Am I supposed to find that comforting?"

"Absolutely not. But I'm not going to sugarcoat things, babe. If I'm not honest, you could die."

She blinked. "Can you handle this?"

"Can you?" he shot back.

"Yes. If you're with me, I feel like I can deal with anything."

His expression softened slightly. "I will be."

"I don't want to be weak."

"You're not. That's admitting you need help. Big difference."

She nodded. "I don't want to be anyone's burden. I don't want to bring danger to anyone."

"Kayla—"

"I got Hoss killed. Don't you understand? He let his guard down because..." She stopped. Bit her lip.

"You were sleeping with him," Teige said bluntly.

"No. We came close. He pulled back. But it was all distracting. I was lonely. He gave me the camera. He got me back into life."

"Or maybe you would've gotten there all on your own."

She narrowed her eyes. "Don't. If you judge Hoss, you judge me."

"Bullshit. He's the one who was paid to protect you. To be professional. If he couldn't handle his feelings and his job, he should've stepped away as your watcher."

"So you can handle both?"

"I've been telling myself that I like the military because war isn't personal. But everything in life is motherfucking personal, and there are some things—some people—who are worth fighting for. I can fall in love with you and protect you. Trust me."

"I do," she told him, a small smile on her lips. "That feels good to admit. I'm tired of not feeling."

"Who's stopping you?"

So much... "Me."

"So unstop." His voice was teasing but his eyes were dead serious. She'd loved those eyes from the moment she'd seen them, a predator's eyes in the dark.

"I can't try."

"I can help."

She glanced at her wrists, the red fading. "Good."

He hugged her, gathered her up and walked her upstairs to the bedroom. He tucked her in before she realized what was happening.

He was putting her to bed. And he was going to leave her. Again. She could see it in his eyes and she fought like hell to stop him from putting her down on the mattress.

"What the fuck, Kayla?"

She clawed at him, until he restrained her and something seized inside her. She stilled, breathed. "Take me."

"You're not thinking straight."

"Because of *you*, Teige."

She'd gone from soft and pliable to fighting again. And she was right—it was his fault. Leaving was what he did best. He'd finally met someone who wasn't letting him get away from it, and she was prepared to fight for him.

Kayla was yanking at him, clawing to keep him with her. Teige hadn't been sure it was the time or place for this, but her battle to get him into bed was something he couldn't resist. She ripped his shirt, stopped and looked surprised for a brief second before tearing it off him completely.

He did the same to her, then began to pull her jeans down as she wrestled with his jeans. After several sweaty minutes, they were naked, kissing, biting, sucking, wanting, needing each other. She was groaning in his mouth, so goddamned wet for him that he slid inside her without warning. She arched up off the bed, calling his name.

And then she wrapped around him and began to move against him.

It was like being in a cage fight, and she was battling a hell of a demon. She fought to roll him onto his back, and he let her. He lay back, held onto her hips to drive her deeper, letting her fuck him. Because she had to. Because he wanted her to, and giving up control like this wasn't easy.

But it was so fucking worth it. The fire in her eyes, the flush of her cheeks, the triumph of learning to let go was simply fucking amazing.

He pinched her nipples and she writhed. He bucked up into her and she slammed him back with a hand around his throat.

She came with a scream. Collapsed on top of him. He waited until her breathing came easily and then, with no warning, he rolled her over and caught her wrists in his hands.

He was still inside her. "It's my turn. Don't you move," he told her.

Chapter 28

ABBY AND JACOBY went back to Kayla's house together. They swept it thoroughly, hoping to find something—anything—the detectives didn't that would show Mara had been there.

But it was clean. Mara was as good as her reputation, Abby supposed. She paced the room and stopped when she heard a creaking upstairs. She looked at Jacoby and they both said, "The damned ghost," at the same time.

She shook her head and laughed. "Dammit, maybe the ghost knows something we don't."

"Can't put him on a witness stand." Jacoby stared at her. "I'll keep things under control here—why don't you take off and get some shut-eye? Decompress. No one's getting to me or Kayla and Teige."

She knew what Teige was capable of and was beginning to have a glimmer of suspicion of what Jacoby could do as well. "I won't be gone long."

"You've been up for forty-eight hours straight. You'll

do well with a nap and a shower. Grab your things and then we'll set up here together," Jacoby told her firmly, pointing to his bag. "That way, we'll be able to take shifts."

It was coming to that. "And Diane?"

Jacoby checked his phone and sent off a quick text. A couple of moments later, a reassuring ding had him nodding. "Safe and sound. No action today. No reports of any strangers in the area."

They were taking a chance by not letting the public know about Mara possibly being in their crosshairs—or vice-versa. But the identical twin concept would make things far too confusing for people, and made it more likely that Mara would stay away. And the point was to lure her in, although certainly not the way Kayla wanted to handle it. "Fine. I'll be an hour, tops."

"Go. I'll order us dinner. And yes, I'll check in with Teige every ten." That was their rule. Mara was dangerous enough to warrant that, and if she had help... "Abby, go," Jacoby pressed gently.

She knew why he was sending her off, and she couldn't blame him. He wanted to see if she could clear her mind, shake off her own demons and come back to the house prepared for whatever might happen.

There's no shame in you not being able to handle this one, Abby. Say the word and you'll be holed up with your brother and Kayla.

In a non-working capacity, of course.

"I won't let him break me—I won't let him win," she whispered fiercely to herself on the ride home. It was the mantra she'd used for years after it happened. Because

Teige was the one who'd reminded her that she'd won, she'd survived. Fought back.

She still could.

She went into her house, stripped out of her clothes and showered, a long hot one to ease her aching muscles. If she slept, it'd be for weeks and she'd rather do it under Jacoby's watchful eye than risk leaving him and Teige and Kayla alone for longer than promised. She packed some clothes and ran her hands through her wet hair to keep it from tangling. It was then that her iPad began to ring.

Ethan. She touched the Facetime screen and Ethan's face appeared, shadowed and backlit. As usual, she could hear the sounds of shelling in the background. He was always in a war zone. Apparently, so was she. "Hey."

"Babe, I've been trying to reach you—what's wrong?"

"Nothing. Everything. Just a problem with work." She desperately wanted to say it was under control, and it was on the tip of her tongue to give him that reassurance, but she couldn't this time. "None of this is good."

"What's not good—us?"

"How would we know anymore? We're never together. I can't have a relationship only on Skype. Correction—I don't want to." It wasn't right to take this out on him—she knew that, but suddenly she didn't give much of a shit.

"It's been tough, I know. I'm almost at the end. We're almost at the end of this."

He'd promised that before, years earlier. After six months at home, he went back out on this job. "I'm so damaged, E," she whispered.

"Not for me. Never for me."

She stared at him through the screen. "I don't know. I..."

"Wait for me, Abs. We'll figure it out. It's always worse when we're not together."

That was true, but this was a long tour for Ethan. She wanted to tell him things, but hell, knowing him, he already knew most everything.

After they'd been together for six months, he'd told her he knew she'd nearly been brutally killed and that she'd seen enough violence to send most people screaming over the edge.

She'd accused him of reading her files until she realized they were under lock and key because she'd been a juvenile. Because it was still a classified, open case. "I've got to go."

"Abs, wait—"

"Tired, Ethan. Really just tired." She hung up on him, then shut her iPad down and silenced her phone. Fuck it. Everyone could deal with not being able to get to her for ten minutes.

In ten minutes, she could pull it all together. And even as she tried to convince herself of that, her hands began to shake. She took a shot of scotch to steady her nerves—because Ethan might be the one with the sight, but she had the knot in the pit of her stomach. And she couldn't tell him that, was convinced, anyway, that it was more about her fears than anything surrounding him.

She eyed the bottle, then pushed it away. She had to be on alert for Kayla. Even though she was staying with Teige, Kayla was her job. Her responsibility.

And Jacoby's. *Can't forget your partner.*

Staying close to Kayla would bring too much suspicion on her under normal circumstances, but these were anything but.

Her bag was packed. She'd stay at Kayla's house while Kayla stayed at Teige's. Mara would surface soon. Diane was being watched, so even if Mara approached her, there was no place to turn.

"No place to hide," she muttered.

"But I don't need to. Not anymore."

Abby whirled around at the sound of the woman's voice, gun drawn...and collapsed. For several sickening seconds, her body writhed helplessly on the ground, out of control as the volts of electricity from the Taser speared through her.

Teige had her Kayla on her hands and knees, her wrists tied, legs spread so wide she was totally off balance, held upright only on his whim.

"You're so tense," he'd murmured against her cheek, his breath tickling her, an oddly gentle sensation that overwhelmed her more than the hard thrusts inside of her.

"Like you wouldn't be," she snapped, and that earned her several slaps on her ass.

"We'll get rid of that."

"Where's the *we*?" she asked. "I don't see you tied up."

"If I was, I couldn't help you like this." His fingers and

mouth were on her again, until she was practically sobbing with need.

"Please, Teige—you have to...I want..."

"What, baby?"

"More. Just...more."

She was begging—and she got what she asked for—more spanking slaps on her ass. At first, she'd started at how the warm flush made her want more. More of his control, his touches...his face, buried between her legs, licking her until she whimpered and half collapsed, begging for him.

Now she accepted that her being helpless and bent to his will turned him on, which turned her on. Giving him control ensured her pleasure. Such a simple power exchange...fueled by her trust, and his voice. He was giving the commands and she was following them. A slave to them and she loved it. Felt free for possibly the first time ever.

This was what she needed.

This would heal her. She didn't know how or why, but the feeling that it would was embedded in her as surely as breathing.

Chapter 29

MARA'S FACE hovered above her. Mara's face—Kayla's face—floating there, smiling, and that made this so much worse. Because Abby knew this was Mara, but Mara had cut her hair, colored it...and she was Kayla in this moment.

Mara knew it too.

When Abby opened her mouth to speak but nothing came out. Mara smiled, almost sympathetically. "The Taser shock will wear off soon enough."

As Abby lay on the floor, dealing with the aftershocks, Mara handcuffed her hands behind her back and dragged her over to the nearest chair. She tied Abby's arms to the back of the chair and lashed her ankles to it as well.

"Did you like the reminders I left for you?" Mara asked, with a casual toss of her hair, like they were girl-friends, comparing makeup tips. When Abby frowned, Mara said impatiently, "At Diane's? I called you to the house to let you know I was there...I didn't expect Diane to have a copy of the Black Magic Killer's autobiography, but

I couldn't resist pulling out the best pages for you." She smiled. "It's one of my favorite books."

Abby felt the sinking in her stomach. "Diane texted us."

"Well, she did, yes. I told her to so technically that was true. That chick would do anything to stay alive and screw my sister over."

"I'd think you wouldn't like that," Abby muttered.

"Well, I've pretty much scarred Diane for life, right? That's something. Better than killing her, I think." Mara shrugged. "She's just a jealous bitch, but she was perfect for what I had planned."

Now that Abby's vision had cleared, she could focus better on Mara. Her hair was the same shade as Kayla's had been dyed—their original color underneath was a honeyed blond—and her eyes were as blue as Kayla's, even more intense with the darker hair color. Their features? Identical. They really were identical. Same height and body type. And for someone who'd been on the run for years, she looked modern and fresh—her makeup was on point, her ripped jeans and black top trendy. She'd turn heads. And her personality was more magnetic than Kayla's—Abby could literally feel her presence fill the room as she bounced around, making herself tea, chatting a mile a minute about the weather, the town, Abby's house...

"Are you okay?" Mara looked concerned, touched Abby's cheek and then moved her fingers down to Abby's neck, where the Taser had hit as Abby tried not to pull away in revulsion at the touches. "Shit, that left a big mark. Sorry about that."

"So don't do it again," Abby managed and Mara gave her a sardonic half smile.

"We've got a lot in common."

"Right. Like what?"

Mara took a sip of her tea. "Claire. My dad. *Hoss*...you know, at first, he thought he was luring me in to capture me," Mara scoffed. "Men are so easy. So stupid when they lead with their dicks."

"Maybe, but women do stupid things all the time in the name of love."

Mara pointed at her. "You and I could've been friends...if this wasn't our destiny."

Mara believed that so badly, it was apparent. And then she told Abby, "You don't know if you trusted the wrong person. I mean, come on, Kayla could've killed Penny way more easily than Mara. Kayla took those pictures. She knew she could easily lure Penny into a trip to the airport with the promise of an audition. And the worst part is, Kayla's been in bed with your brother. Did you bring evil into his life because you're obsessed with evil? I know all about you from Hoss. He shared everything."

Bile rose in her throat. "Did he know...?" she managed to mouth.

"Who I was? Of course. I helped him pick out the camera that got Kayla motivated again—from what I've seen, she's getting lots of use out of it. And he was helping me prove that Claire belongs behind bars, not me." She tilted her head to the side. "You don't seem surprised.

"I'm not surprised by anything men do," Abby said flatly, her voice hoarse and strange to her own ears.

"Is that man you were talking to a cheater too?" Mara asked. "They all are, honey. They can't help it—we can either accept it and have our own fun or get mad all the time. And I'm tired of being mad."

Abby couldn't help it—she laughed.

"I know—you must think I'm angry all the time and that's why I've killed." Mara sighed. "It's part of it, but most of the time, I'm a very even person."

Charming, even, Abby thought to herself. Just like Kayla had mentioned—Abby could definitely see Mara with a large group of friends around. "Kayla...she talks about you a lot.

"Claire, you mean? She's always tried to outsmart me." Mara shrugged. "I'm so many steps ahead of her...because right now, she's waiting for me. She's making herself bait. Luring me. But I'm way more interested in the friends she's finally made."

"I'm not her friend," Abby snapped.

"No, I wouldn't think you'd like her very much," Mara mused. "She tends to bite the hand that feeds her, right?"

Abby nodded, because going along with Mara was her best chance of staying alive long enough to be found. "I've noticed. She's difficult."

Mara laughed. "You're not sure if agreeing with me is going to piss me off or get me on your side, so you're trying to be diplomatic."

It was Abby's turn to shrug. "You're family. Family's always complicated as hell."

"True." Mara frowned. "If she'd just come to me before

this..." Then she waved her hand. "Forget it. Past is past, no matter what they say."

"Is it though, for you? Because you seem to be constantly reliving it."

Mara waggled a finger at her. "Touché, Marshal Daniels."

"But Claire doesn't know much about it."

"Or so she claims." Mara countered, checking her watch. "I won't lose track of the time, by the way. Talk or not, you'll be dead before anyone can help you."

Abby's gut tightened and she forced herself to ignore the end of Mara's sentence. "You really think she's that good of a liar? Because I've seen through all the lies she's told me. She'd have to go a long way to pretend to be an amnesiac."

Her words sounded casual to her own ears. Despite the bindings, she tried to keep her muscles loose, her pose as relaxed as it could be, hearing Dad's voice in her head.

Every killer messes up at some point. You've just got to pray it's on your watch.

Chapter 30

IN THE AFTERMATH, Teige lay on his back with Kayla curled against his side. "Did I wear you out?"

She glanced up at him. "I'm just getting started, old man."

"Really—we're going there?" He laughed. "You think I'll have trouble keeping up with you?"

"I guess we'll have to see."

"You don't know what I'm capable of. I don't even know...at least I didn't..." she whispered.

"And now?"

"Now I'm willing to find out." She bit her bottom lip.

"I definitely know what you're capable of," he told her, his voice husky, his cock already hard for her again. "But if you want to try to surprise me, go for it."

She gave him a shy smile...but he knew there was something devious behind it. "Has anyone ever tied you up?"

"Sure." He paused, then frowned. "Wait—you mean in bed?"

That made her smile. "That's what I was thinking of, yes."

"Oh. Then no." He frowned. "That's what you want?"

"You said to surprise you."

"That'll teach me to be talking in bed instead of fucking," he muttered. Then, before he could back out, he grabbed for the ropes he'd tied her with and handed them over to her.

She hesitated—briefly—until he forced them into her hands.

"Come on," he said roughly. "You're not going to get this chance often. I'd take advantage of it while I'm feeling generous."

"Suppose I end up liking it this way?"

He had no doubt she probably could. He could always see the wild girl hidden behind the shy one—the anger only served to tuck that wild side away, because Kayla was ashamed of it, assumed that the wild girl was the reason for so many of her troubles.

It was exactly the opposite—that part of Kayla had been what helped her survive.

She bit her lip as she straddled him and tied his wrists together, and then to the headboard, just like he'd done to her. It took him extra concentration—and a few internal curses—to make sure he didn't rip his arms from the bonds.

"Are you going to be okay?" she asked as she watched him.

He glanced up at his arms, stretched out overhead. "You didn't tie them too tight."

"That's not what I mean." She flipped her hair so it hung heavily over one shoulder. Her voice was a little husky—a little excited seeing him tied, and he got that. That's what it was all about for him. "You don't let this happen often."

"At all," he corrected. "It's not my thing. But if you want to experience it from my side, I'm okay with that."

"Good. God, I can see why you like this." She ran her palms up his arms as she thrust against him, like she was reveling in her power. "Why aren't you scared of me?"

"Why should I be?"

"Hoss trusted Mara—he trusted her over me."

"Don't really care to discuss either one at the moment."

"Don't you see? He trusted a serial killer over me—he believed I could hurt people."

"You're no different than anyone, Kayla. We can all hurt others. But in the part of your life you remember— from the hospital after the fire onward—you haven't killed anyone, have you?"

"No," she managed.

"You're thinking too fucking much instead of taking this opportunity to fuck me. Because trust me, if you don't start doing something, I'm going to turn you over my knee —" She stopped his talking mid-breath by squeezing his nipples with her thumb and forefinger—hard—and then bending down to bite one. Then she was alternately biting and sucking them, and his chest, his neck...leaving a trail of wet red marks...

She was marking him. There would be bruises when she was done, but the pain/pleasure line had always been finely blurred for him. He was hard. He wanted more. He wanted her—and only her—and he'd beg for her in a way he'd never begged anyone.

"Come on, babe, just fuck me," he growled as she fisted his cock in her cool palm, teasing him, sucking his balls, biting the insides of his thighs until his muscles screamed at the tension.

Finally—fucking finally—she was giving in, sliding herself down on him, rocking back and forth, lost in the pleasure of the moment...but never breaking his gaze.

Hell, he loved her. He was tied up, with a knife on the table and he was vulnerable as fuck. And he stayed like that, although he stilled when she leaned over to grab the knife. She opened it, and the blade hovered above him.

He was still inside of her when she cut the ropes off—and she was still moving as she told him, "I want you to hold me when I come."

She didn't have to ask twice. He tugged her chest to his, held her tightly as she lost it in his arms, milking his cock with her orgasm until he came hard...and this time, he was the one yelling her name.

Mara picked the biggest knife out of Abby's butcher block, much in the way Abby always imagined the Black Magic Killer doing. She found it ironic, of course, that her father had been killed with his own kitchen utensils, but that hadn't stopped her from putting her own identical butcher block in her kitchen. She'd figured it would balance karma.

Abby, zero; karma, a true bitch, was the winner.

"You don't want to do this," Abby told her, because it was the only thing she could think of. It was also the stupidest. Of course, Mara wanted to—was compelled to—and the only way to stop it would be if someone got here in time.

"You're wrong about that," Mara said flatly as she stared at herself in the thick, shiny blade before putting it down on the counter she leaned a hip against, then crossed her arms. She noted Abby's glance between her and the knife and simply smiled. "You watched your father get killed by the Black Magic Killer."

"Yes. I watched it happen." Abby couldn't tell for sure, but that might've actually gained her a certain level of respect in Mara's eyes.

"You didn't look away?"

"Not once." She'd wanted to, but the Black Magic Killer told her it would go easier on her father if she listened to him.

Of course, it had all been a lie. The killing couldn't have been any more brutal, but looking away would've made Abby's father die alone and she couldn't have that.

"Was it messy?" Mara asked as she picked up the knife and approached.

Abby stiffened. "It's blurry—like it happened very fast and somehow very slow too." As Abby spoke, Mara leaned forward and began to unbutton Abby's shirt. She pushed it back away and off Abby's shoulders, exposing some of the scars on her belly, remnants from the Black Magic Killer that would never fade completely.

"And he almost killed you," Mara continued as she ran a fingertip along the scars, tracing them like they were a map, and then she ran the tip of the knife along one. Abby stared, watching the blood swell up from the cut.

At first, she felt nothing and then Mara dug the knife in harder, literally opening the old wound.

Abby's mouth opened and a sharp cry escaped. Mara smiled, and followed the scar with the knife to the one that led up to Abby's shoulder. She used the knife to rip open the arm of the shirt, then repeated, "And he almost killed you, right?" She jabbed the knife into Abby's shoulder and Abby jolted.

"He tried his best." Her belly was wet with blood, and she was numb. Even so, she could practically feel his hands on her ankles, yanking her back. She smelled the smoke, the blood, her voice raw from screaming...

Mara was bending down, lifting Abby's pants up to look at her ankles and calves, where there were scars from his nails—she had divots in her skin from him digging in to hold her and pull her toward him. Scars that proved she'd fought for her life—and won.

Would she be that lucky again?

Mara dug the tip of the knife into Abby's ankle a few times, then glanced up at her. "How did you escape?"

Abby tilted her head back, letting a sob that came out more like a hiss escape. "We all have our stories." She forced her gaze to Mara's. "Why don't you tell me your story, Mara? I could record it all, for posterity. It would be a bestseller."

They both knew that was the truth. Mara shrugged but she looked pleased.

Abby held her breath, knowing she had to buy time. It was the only thing she had in her control. "I think Claire was wrong about you."

Mara sat on the floor, holding the bloody knife. "Why? What did she say about me?"

"She talked about you all the time. How you took all the blame for everything."

"She remembered that?"

Abby nodded. "And she wasn't planning on doing a damned thing about it."

Mara picked up the knife as she stood, then grabbed a flashlight off the counter. She shined the light directly into Abby's eyes, a cop move for sure, and Abby lost track of the knife immediately.

"Did you ever wonder if you're wrong?" Mara asked slyly. "Claire's been running from me, can't remember anything...she's in your good graces..."

Abby was tied too tightly to move. She blinked against the harsh light Mara shined directly into her eyes and tried to stave off the impending panic Mara was intent on causing. "What are you trying to say, Mara? I'm not in the mood for riddles." She didn't bother to hide the irritability in her voice from Mara.

Mara, not Kayla—Abby had to focus on that, not let Mara make her question her instincts. It didn't matter how alike they looked and sounded, how many times Mara told her that she and Kayla were in on this together, from the start.

Abby locked her mind against Mara's head games and tried to play one of her own. "Why are you so interested in the Black Magic Killer?"

"Ah Abby, don't disappoint me now." Mara sighed. "The Black Magic Killer was my father."

Abby swallowed hard. There was no goddamned way that was possible—none at all. The dates didn't match up, according to the records Abby had seen on Mara's early family life, but the Black Magic Killer hadn't been heard of again after the night he'd almost killed Abby. One theory was that he'd died of smoke inhalation after the fact, but had escaped far enough away for the body not to have been tied to the scene or recovered.

When Abby spoke again, her voice was calm, almost condescending. "Your father was an old drunk, not a famed serial killer. I have DNA proof that he's not," Abby lied.

"You don't know what you're talking about," Mara said firmly, but there had been the very briefest of falters when she spoke. "You know, I've never loved the slow bleed-out method, but I can see it has its uses." She ran the knife along Abby's shoulder scar again, digging in deeper and following it down to Abby's belly and even so, Abby couldn't see a damned thing because of the light, could only feel the burning, unable to tell exactly how deep the knife was cutting.

She forced herself to ask, "Did you start killing because you thought you'd make him proud?" in hopes of distracting her.

Mara laughed, almost manically out of control—and extremely chilling—and for a moment, Abby regretted asking. She shut the light off, and Abby blinked to find her leaning across the table, the knife inches from Abby's face. "I guess there's no harm in telling you. It's a shame that you won't be able to travel the country, lecturing about this, right? But don't worry—I'm writing my own book. I'll make sure you're immortalized properly."

"Doing things properly is important to you."

"Very. If more people did things the way they were supposed to, if people acknowledged what they were supposed to..."

"Like Kayla?"

"It's cute how you insist on calling her the wrong name. She can't stand it."

Mara was so completely, utterly believable.

"Anyway," Mara waved her hand. "My father deserved the fame he got. If he'd been able to continue, well, those were circumstances that couldn't be helped. I kept up his work. It's not something I'd expected to do but..." She shrugged. "I guess it's in my blood."

"What are the circumstances?" Abby pressed.

Mara glanced up at her slyly, rising to the challenge. "There are things you don't know."

"I know you're angry at Kayla—you keep telling everyone she's a murderer. Is that simply wishful thinking? Guilty conscience?"

Mara went to Abby's fridge, poured herself a glass of iced tea and sat across from Abby to drink it. Just two old friends, having sweet tea and gossiping. "It freaks you out, how much I look like her, right?"

"Does it freak you out?"

"Can we just converse without you trying to turn everything around on me?" Mara sounded exasperated, like a mother lecturing a child. Not like a killer who'd tied up a US Marshal.

"You're right." Abby nodded. "Tell me about the secret Ka—Claire's not telling anyone."

Mara nodded approvingly at the name change. "Claire's a very good secret-keeper. She's kept up the amnesia story quite well. I'm so proud of her for that. At times, I almost think she believes it herself."

"I think you're right. So you think she hasn't been honest with us?" Abby lowered her voice conspiratorially, figuring she'd get Tased again for being so blatant.

But Mara was so concrete—and thrilled to be discussing Claire, and getting her own story in there. Abby knew the jurors probably wouldn't have cared to discuss any of this. Not that it would've saved them anyway.

What's going to save you?

She shook that out of her mind—no reason to go there. *Don't worry about what you can't change, just change what you can*, Dad would say. "I know you're stronger than Claire. She's had a tough time these past years."

"Claire's always needed taking care of. But she's definitely got our dad's blood in her. She didn't realize it. I'm sure she regrets it, now that she knows how much power Dad had."

Abby nodded diligently.

"So she's really never mentioned this?"

"Just the amnesia."

"Right." Mara shook her head like she was getting confused. "Do you have any Advil? I'm getting a terrible headache."

"Cabinet next to the fridge."

Mara got the pills, took several and washed them down with more sweet tea. Then she smiled, leaned in too close for Abby's comfort before sharing, "Claire killed Daddy." Abby was still trying to process the fact that Kayla might've killed her own father when Mara said, "I didn't see it happen," very matter of factly. "If I'd been there, none of it would've happened, so I definitely take responsibility for it."

"You're sure? Why would she do that?"

"Daddy always visited my bedroom. That night, Claire was in my bed but he didn't know that."

Abby's stomach recoiled at how easily Mara recounted what seemed to amount to sexual abuse...and seemed to be acting as if it was somehow consensual on her part. Or, at the very least, not something that bothered her. "Did Claire know?"

"No, I didn't think she needed to know. She wasn't as strong as I was, or as close to Daddy. But I think she got upset. She told me that Dad touched her, and then said she stabbed him because it was the only way she could think of to stop him. She'd been cutting out some paper dolls, so the scissors were on the nightstand." Mara shrugged. "He was dead. She stabbed him in the neck—just a lucky break on her part. I needed to save Claire from getting in trouble, so I took care of everything."

Abby felt the bile rise in her throat. She wanted to ask more, but she couldn't put words to the horror that Mara had unfolded for her.

Fortunately—or not—she didn't have to say anything else. Mara was comfortable now, only too happy to talk. "So I killed Mom—that wasn't a hardship. I used Daddy's gun and then I set the piece of shit double-wide on fire. I saved Claire and then watched her become damned ungrateful for it over time."

Abby caught on to that immediately. "You said Claire worked with you."

Mara looked at her, a gaze so chilling that Abby knew, once and for all, that Kayla was Kayla and Mara was Mara...there was no way Kayla could've hidden that inside of her for so long.

Mara stood now, Taser in hand. "You all think you're so smart, but trust me, you're not. Not at all. Claire will learn to appreciate what I've done for her, and she'll learn to love honoring our father's legacy."

"He's not the Black Magic Killer. I've seen the Black Magic Killer, Mara. I was face to face with him. Do you think I'd ever forget that man?" Abby's voice shook, more anger than fear as Mara came closer. "I saw pictures of your father. I know the whole story," Abby lied, recalling the queries in the CPS report and hoping to hit the nail on the head. "Your father was a alcoholic pedophile who fucked you because you were too stupid to know the difference between a renowned serial killer and a drunk."

Harsh words she would never say to any other victim of childhood abuse, unless they were complete psychopathic monsters, like the woman in front of her.

It got Abby the reaction she'd been hoping for. Mara lunged and, at the same time, Abby slammed up and head-butted her, hard enough to knock herself, still in the chair, to the floor and Mara backward. Mara stumbled, hit her head on the corner of the table and went still on the ground.

She was knocked out, but it wouldn't be for long. Abby was still trapped. She thumped the chair over to the hallway, where her phone was, used her nose to type something to Teige. Three numbers—and it took her typing an entire string of them. With no way to delete, because of time, she sent the string, hoping he'd see what he needed to.

Because Mara was stirring. And she'd be pissed—and wouldn't fall for the same trick twice.

"Mara, if we make a call, we can get you on the news," she promised as Mara rolled onto her hands and knees, then grabbed for the edge of the table.

"You don't even believe in my legacy," she pointed out.

"Convince me."

Mara came up to her and smiled, a sweet smile, right before she put the Taser on the side of Abby's neck again.

Chapter 31

TEIGE STARED AT THE PHONE, still in a post-sex haze. That ended the second he saw the old code texted from Abby and he was in full command, throwing clothes on and out the door, yelling for Kayla to get in the car and getting Jacoby on the line.

"This could be a trap," Teige told him. "She punched in a million numbers, so she could've tried to get lucky."

"Or she could be tied up," Jacoby offered.

"She wouldn't give that code up for anything. She wouldn't lead me to my death. She'd die first."

Jacoby was silent for a long moment. "That I believe."

———

On her way out the door, Kayla had grabbed her phone and tripped over her camera's strap. The case was lying on the floor and Kayla grabbed it up without thinking and joined Teige in the truck.

Once Jacoby told them to get a block from Abby's house and just goddamned wait, which went over with Teige well, Kayla sat rigidly next to him, not sure of what to say. The camera and case were worn from use—Hoss had gotten it for her years earlier. And while this wasn't a photo opportunity, somehow it was the only link she had to Hoss...to Mara.

She didn't tell Teige that she'd started to feel the shivers down her spine. Mara was close—they knew that. But maybe Mara was closer than she'd ever thought.

She turned the case over in her lap, the fabric soft against her thighs. She brushed away what she thought was a white piece of lint but it didn't come off.

She looked closer. Unzipped the case. When she pressed the thin fabric in her fingers it almost crinkled.

"What's wrong?" Teige asked.

"Nothing. It's...maybe these are directions." It was inane, she knew—they were driving to save Abby and she was worried about a camera case, but it had been placed in front of her. Maybe it was Old Man Kennen, making a trip next door. Hoss, from beyond the grave, good old fate...or maybe she'd finally opened her eyes and began to look around for her place in all of this.

She tried to pull the fabric delicately at first, and then she ended up ripping it open. There was a folded piece of paper in there, and when she opened it, there was a child's handwriting—crayon—on a full sheet of loose-leaf paper. It was yellowed with age...and it was Mara's handwriting. She gasped and said, "Teige, there's a note in here..."

"For you?" he asked as he barreled down the street,

pulling onto the curb a block from Abby's house. She read him the note—he cursed and then Jacoby joined them, jumping into the back seat of the truck almost before it stopped moving.

"What's going on?" Jacoby asked, noting the stunned atmosphere. She passed the note to him and he read it. "Is this shit you know?"

"Maybe," she whispered.

The journal entry was dated two days after the fire. It was done in awkward crayon, on the back of a generic blank hospital nursing notes form used in patient binders.

I killed for Claire because she killed for me first. And then I set the fire to make sure she wouldn't get blamed for any of it.

"It doesn't feel like an alibi. Or a lie. It's like a confession. A secret," Kayla murmured, even as something inside her brain began to stir. "I know she's told me this, but I don't have any memory the fire, or of getting out of the house. She waited until it nearly burned to the ground and we had smoke inhalation. I guess she did that purposely, to hide the evidence and make us look innocent. Everyone knew we were abused, so the fact that they were passed out when the fire started wasn't a surprise. The bones were so burned and they didn't do an autopsy." Kayla paused. "I remember waking up in an ambulance on the lawn. The smell of smoke. Barely being able to breathe."

"Before that?"

"Going to school and getting in trouble. But the psychologist told me that happened days before the fire. I depended on Mara's memories for all of that. I believed everything she told me."

"And now?"

"I think she might not have told me the whole story."

"Guess not," Jacoby muttered. "So why is it in this case? When did it get put there?"

"Hoss gave me this camera after I'd been his witness for about six months. Long before Mara killed him," she said quietly.

"And this is the case he gave you?" Teige asked.

"Yes."

"Was the camera found in the room where Hoss was killed?" Jacoby asked.

"No," Teige said, and Abby concurred. "It was with me, in the darkroom, where I was developing pictures. Hoss had set the space up for me right after he'd given me the camera..."

Teige and Jacoby exchanged a look between them and Kayla's stomach twisted when she held up the camera and said, "This is how she's known how to find me. There's got to be a tracker in here. Hoss knew it when he gave it to me. And she's always known...every time I take a picture, she gets a step closer to hurting me."

Teige lunged out of the truck but Jacoby was already there, meeting him at the driver's door, ready to stop him.

"Move the fuck out of my way," he told Jacoby, and when the man didn't move, he shoved him hard to the side.

But Jacoby didn't shove all that easily, shot his arm out to hold Teige back against the truck. "You're not thinking clearly."

Teige didn't want to think—he wanted action. He pushed at Jacoby and the men wrestled to the point of nearly falling to the ground after slamming against the truck multiple times.

Jacoby finally panted, "You want a neighbor to see this, call the police and spook Mara into killing Abby?"

And that made Teige rip himself from Jacoby's grasp. He forced himself still, ignoring the overwhelming urge to still make a break for it. "I couldn't help her the night she almost died. I need to help her now."

"I know that," Jacoby assured him. "Let's get eyes and ears on what's happening first—rushing in's a way for people to get killed. And if Mara's been this far ahead of us, she might have the house wired."

It was true—and something Teige would normally have thought of, had the case not been so personal to him. "How do we proceed."

"Let me go in," Kayla told both of them. Neither man had realized she'd gotten out of the car, and she stood there now, her voice pleading. "Let me help. That's what she wants."

"Exactly—she wants to hurt you and Abby—and I'm not letting that happen," Teige told her, then turned to Jacoby. "I'll go in through the goddamned roof."

Jacoby started to speak but Kayla cut him off. "You both need to listen to me—"

"No," they both told her simultaneously, then went

back to their arguing about who was going to storm the house first.

"I'm going in—I have the experience. I do this shit for a living," Teige told him, and Jacoby finally conceded.

And then... "Shit—the neighbors," Jacoby said through gritted teeth as he waved toward an older guy who was coming down the walkway. "We're okay, sir. Just a bit of a misunderstanding between friends."

"You two get the hell out of here," the man told them. "I'll call 9-1-1 if you two aren't gone by the time I count to five."

You two...

It was at that moment they realized Kayla was gone.

Chapter 32

IT TOOK Abby longer to move this time—Mara had amped the Taser voltage and Abby's muscles jerked painfully, then continued to ache as she tried to keep track of Mara, who was pacing around her prone body. Abby was still attached to the chair, her arms yanked behind her uncomfortably as she attempted to force her body to move.

Wasn't happening. And Mara just stood there and watched her struggle. Even laughed a few times, which made Abby so goddamned mad she actually did manage to move.

Once that happened, Mara grabbed the chair and yanked it upright, hard enough to make Abby's neck jerk uncomfortably.

"Don't fuck with me, Abby. Maybe you escaped one killer, but lightning doesn't strike twice."

"And yet here I am, fighting off another serial killer. I'd say those are one-in-a-million odds," Abby choked out, her voice raw.

"I guess about as good as the odds of a serial killer spawning two murderers. Claire was always a bad seed. No one ever saw that."

"She admitted as much."

"And still managed to appear innocent."

"Because she didn't murder anyone," Abby shot back. "You're insane if you believe that."

"And that's where you're wrong."

"You have proof? Because the trial would've been the time to do that." Mara had the knife again, menacing Abby with it, and Abby hated this part, the power play, the fear, the control. "What will this do?" Abby asked tiredly. "What will killing me actually do, Mara?"

"Close the circle. I'll finish my dad's job."

"And Claire?"

Mara smiled at something over Abby shoulder. "It looks like she'll help."

Abby turned her neck as much as she could and looked up to see Kayla standing behind her, an icy look in her eyes.

You can always tell us apart by our eyes.

But in this moment, Abby couldn't. Her heart beat a tattoo against her ribs and she took some deep breaths so she didn't vomit right there. Because Kayla had a knife... and she held it casually against the side of Abby's neck. When Abby had turned, she felt it press into her skin.

"There's already blood on her knife," Mara pointed out happily.

"What did you do, Kayla?" Abby demanded.

"It's Claire. And shut up," Kayla told her.

The eyes, they weren't helping... "Don't—"

"Do you want the honors?" Mara asked Kayla.

"Together. It's the best way."

"You know what you did, right, Claire?" Mara asked her. "You killed Daddy. I had to protect you, but you didn't care."

"I didn't remember," Kayla corrected.

"You still could've believed me." Mara grew more agitated with each passing second and was holding that big knife too close for Abby's comfort.

"Tell me what happened, Mara," Kayla demanded.

"She said you killed your father," Abby said, and was rewarded with Mara's fist against her cheekbone. She heard a crack, more arguing and she just tried to keep track of the chaos around her.

"That's not true," Kayla said, her voice rising to an almost hysterical level. "Is it true, Mara? Why didn't you tell me this before? Why keep it from me?"

"I'm protecting you, dammit! That's all I've ever tried to do, and you keep punishing me for it," Mara slammed back. "I killed for you because you killed for me first!"

Kayla's head swam but she forced herself to keep it together. It wasn't just her life that was in danger—more than that, it was Abby's, Teige's sister, and she could never forgive herself if anything happened to her.

Just then, she noticed the smell of smoke in the air. Abby did too and Mara smiled. "I lit a fire upstairs. A slow-burning one, but still, I thought maybe it would jog your memory, Claire. Because I lit the fire at our house that night too."

"You killed our parents."

"No, I covered our crimes—they were already dead," Mara told her. "I kept this secret—your secret—for a long time, but now you need to know what you did. I have Abby as a witness."

"And after you tell me?" Kayla asked.

"Then you kill Abby and we run, together." Mara nodded and Kayla forced herself to lie with a nod. "Good. I want you to think about that day—we'd gone to school, come home, foraged for our supper since Mom was drunk and Dad had been gone for three days."

"Your father, the genius serial killer?" Abby asked boldly.

Kayla hit her in the back of the head, hard enough for Abby's head to jerk forward but not hard enough to cause her real pain, although she groaned just the same. "Keep going, Mara."

"You'd had a bad dream, so you crawled into my bed," Mara told her as Kayla clawed her own mind for access to the memories. "You wanted hot milk, and I'd hidden away some Parmalat that I'd stolen a couple of days earlier. I thought you were safe since he'd been gone for so long. I pulled a chair up to the stove and stood on it so I could watch the pan. You didn't like it when the milk scorched and formed a skin, so I was careful."

That struck a nerve... "I never liked it like that, no," she said quietly.

Mara nodded her approval and continued. "I didn't hear anything. I might've been humming or daydreaming, but either way, I'd let my guard down. It was only after I poured the milk into a mug that I heard the loud thump, the muffled sobs, the sound of you retching. I dropped the milk and ran for my room, because you were in the wrong bed. My bed."

"Why would that matter? Did we used to get in trouble for sleeping in each other's rooms?" Kayla asked.

"I made sure you never had to deal with Dad's kind of trouble," Mara said coldly, and an awareness washed over Kayla like an icy hug. "I found him on the floor, the scissors sticking out of his chest. You were rocking on the floor, your chest over your bent legs, vomit in front of you. When I pulled you up, I saw the blood on the bed—a small, lighter stain—and I knew exactly what had happened."

"You knew..." was all Kayla could say.

Mara finished for her. "I knew because it happened to me all the time. But never to you. Because I always made sure you were never in my bed when he was home."

"Mara—"

"You asked me, 'Did he do this to you? Did he touch you?' and I told you yes, he did. But before we could do anything, Mom was yelling. She lurched into the room and saw Dad. She yelled..."

"Holy Mary Mother of God, what did you do," Kayla said before she could stop herself.

"Yes, that's exactly what she said. And you said—"

"I did it," Kayla said, as woodenly as she had that night. "He touched me."

"Mom slapped you—called you a liar. And I stepped in front of you, Claire, and I told her—"

"He's been doing this to me for years and you've never believed me." Kayla stared at her sister as she spoke her mother's words, "You shut up, you stupid shit. You killed him. What am I gonna do now?"

"She left the room and I took you with me, away from Dad's body. I sat with you in the messy, dirty kitchen area of that shitty double-wide we called home for a few minutes before going to find Mom. If she was going to call the police, I needed to get my story straight. But she was packing. *Packing.* And only her clothes. Muttering, 'Got to get out of here. Welfare will take care of those brats. Gonna get blamed for this.'"

"She was leaving us," Kayla said hollowly.

"You'd already killed to protect yourself, but I knew you'd killed when you realized that Dad had done this to me before."

"It was too familiar to him," Kayla agreed, trying not to throw up as she caught a memory's whiff of his dirty shirt and beer breath as he lay on top of her, telling her, "Give it up easily for Daddy, because you know that's how I like it."

"I went back into the bedroom, yanked the scissors out of Dad's chest. Walked into Mom's room. She screamed when she saw me, but I moved fast, jabbed her, once in the chest, the way you did to our father. I held them there while Mom gurgled something, until she started falling to the floor. And you were watching the whole damned thing from the doorway, after I'd told you to stay put."

"I was worried about you."

"You went into shock. I shoved you away, got the gasoline and poured it on Mom and I set the fire. I stayed in the house with you until the fire spread and the smoke got thick in our lungs. Only then did I dial 9-1-1, yelled 'Help' into the receiver and pulled you onto the lawn."

"You wanted us to have an alibi."

"No one would ever believe we killed our parents, Claire. They knew CPS visited—they all knew how we lived. It wasn't a big stretch to think two drunks fell asleep with cigarettes burning and nearly killed their two innocent daughters," Mara spat. "I remember when the house burned down. I relive it every night—the sweet smell of smoke, the way my heart beat so fast when I saw the flames. For the first time ever, it all seemed right and I knew I'd done the best thing. You hugged me on the lawn. I wrapped a blanket around your shoulders and you looked at me and I looked at you and we didn't need to say anything more, because we both knew what we'd done for each other. Except you forgot."

With that, Mara lunged, knife out. The smoke had gotten thicker—Kayla hadn't realized her eyes were burning until she faced her sister. She yanked Abby's chair out of the way, throwing her to the ground where the smoke was thinner, and she held the knife out toward Mara.

"Don't," she told her sister. "Don't you try to fool me again."

"What are you talking about? You remember—"

"Yes, I remember. I remember that Mom was dead first. She was already dead, and you told me it was an accident, to go lie down in your room until you figured out what to do. I was already in shock and you set me up. You knew Dad was coming home, where he'd go, what he'd try to do."

"I was protecting you," Mara protested coldly.

"You were dragging me in. You killed first and it wasn't self-defense. Maybe I did kill our father, but it was definitely in self-defense. Killing you will be for the same reason." She walked quickly toward Mara and Mara toward her, a game of chicken neither could fully win.

Just when Kayla thought Mara would walk right into her knife, Mara stopped short of it, but Kayla didn't stop moving. It plunged into Mara's stomach and Mara stared down at it and back up at Kayla in disbelief. Mara blinked, eyes watering...maybe from the smoke or maybe not, because she sounded sad when she said, "It doesn't matter. All this time, I thought it would, but it doesn't. I did all of it for you, which means I did it all for nothing."

With that, Kayla let go of the knife's handle. Mara turned, lunged to open the door into the next room. Flames had engulfed the area and she walked directly into them as Kayla screamed—just screamed as Mara cried out and flailed, her body quickly covered in fire.

Kayla watched the body spin and burn...waited until it dropped to the ground before she dragged Abby out of the house.

Chapter 33

TEIGE AND JACOBY had watched the whole thing. Letting Kayla remain in there alone with Mara and an incapacitated Abby was risky as fuck, especially once Jacoby noted that Mara had started a fire some time ago. But they ducked in the mudroom, forced to listen, bear witness to the incredibly painful scene.

Teige wanted Kayla to remember—stopping it all too soon could put her into more shock, more doubt. She needed to know about her past, to know she'd done nothing wrong.

Mara was always the bad seed—she'd just used Kayla as her excuse. Teige would spend as long as it took convincing Kayla of that.

They'd helped take the women out—the ambulance and fire trucks pulling up as they did.

"Body inside the dining room," Jacoby told the fire-fighters. "She's the arsonist." Then he was helping Teige cut the bindings from Abby's arms as the paramedics gave all of them oxygen. Jacoby insisted Abby go to the hospital for treatment.

Kayla had grabbed Teige on the way to the hospital, and as the truck followed Abby's ambulance, she relived her memories. Teige had been surprised to hear Kayla remembering the order of the killings—Mara doing the killing first, in cold blood, changed everything, and Mara couldn't hold on to the reality she had for so long. Mara had wanted Kayla to remember, to be grateful to her, but in getting her wish, Kayla had broken her.

Kayla not remembering Mara's so-called protection was a blow, but Kayla's knowing that Mara killed first and set her up was the final straw.

Would Mara have killed if she hadn't been abused? Impossible to say, but even with the first murders, she could've stopped there. But either that event triggered the illness or she'd liked the killing. Or serial killing was in her blood.

"If I'd remembered sooner..."

"Nothing would've changed, Kayla," Teige told her fiercely.

"Yes, it would've," she shot back just as fiercely. "That bitch would've killed herself sooner and saved innocent lives."

Teige stared at her, then nodded. "You saved my sister."

"She saved me first. Both of you. All of you." And then she collapsed in his arms. "It's over, Teige. And somehow it won't be done for a really long time. I don't know what to do with myself."

"Be grateful you survived. Give back. It's all you can do."

Abby was seen by the doctors immediately in the ER—Teige followed behind her, leaving Kayla in Jacoby's capable hands in order to get another breathing treatment for mild smoke inhalation.

Abby's was worse, exaggerated because of her injuries. There was always the chance of infection, never mind the fact that some of the wounds might be deeper than they looked.

"Sir—"

"I'm her brother," Teige told the doctor.

Abby reached out for his hand. "I'm all right, Teige."

"No, you're not, Abs." His voice broke. "Christ, again..."

"Don't do this because of what happened that night."

Teige knew his eyes were as haunted as hers. "If I was any later...fuck...if I'd been ten minutes earlier..."

"Stop," Abby said firmly. "You saved me. It wasn't your job to save Dad. He put us in so much danger. He knew it and he didn't care."

"He cared, Abs. He just didn't know how to stop hunting or profiling like that. It's as much of an addiction as the killer has, you know? If you don't have that kind of addictive personality, you won't be an effective profiler."

"Takes one to know one," she offered softly. "There's a monster in all of us. We just let it out in different ways."

"So you don't think we were cursed?"

"Of course we are. No getting out of it. But I think I might actually be as lucky as you are." He laughed when she said it and she tried to laugh and said, "Damn, that hurts," her voice quiet.

"Hurts to live, Abs."

Abby gave him a smile, her countenance calm. "I won't let that stop me. Now get the hell out of here and check on my witness while the docs put me back together."

Kayla was just hanging up the phone with Abby when Teige got home. He'd insisted on going back to the hospital to see his sister, and Kayla cuddled with Hanny and the breathing treatments she'd been sent home with.

It was the first time in forever that she'd been alone— although being with Hanny, who didn't leave her side, didn't exactly constitute alone—without worrying if the lights were all on, if the doors were locked, if she was safe.

No one was ever truly safe, but her biggest nightmare had ended. She might still have bad dreams and other issues because of all she'd dealt with, but she was going to be okay.

Especially if she was greeted by Teige's not often seen smile. "Hey babe—things okay?" he asked as he dropped a shopping bag by the couch.

"Abby called to let me know you were on your way. She said she's doing fine." She dug her hands into Hanny's fur and rubbed. "I heard she kicked you out."

He gave a small, unabashed shrug. "She kicked Jacoby out too."

"I think we all need some downtime—and sleep," she said. The four of them had spent the afternoon talking to various members of law enforcement, including members of the FBI who'd known Teige and Abby's dad, agents who'd been working on and studying Mara's case from the start. This case would always remain famous—or infamous —probably more for the way it ultimately ended than anything else.

Teige settled in next to her and Hanny. "Anything you want to talk about before I take you upstairs?"

"Like my memory coming back?" The doctors had told her that it could happen under times of extreme duress, but she'd had so many of those moments without so much as a flash that she'd given up hope. And honestly, having her memory back was a mixed blessing, because it forced her to deal with everything she never had. Abby had told her tonight that they'd "discuss our pasts over wine until it's all out of our systems" and Kayla planned on taking her up on it.

"Like that, yeah." He reached out to rub the back of her neck.

"There were times she'd come into my room. I rarely slept at night, even then. I knew something was wrong and she did too—she'd come in when I had nightmares and even then, most of the time I'd ignore her. Brush her off. Ignore how hurt she looked. And I realize that, no matter what signs were there, there's nothing I could've done. It was all on her. She would've kept going after the people who got close to me until she got what she wanted."

"And you know what that was now?" he asked.

"Yes. She wanted me to be the one who stopped her. She wanted me to feel the guilt."

"Do you?"

She shook her head and reached for his hand. "I feel free. I am free. I have no regrets."

"Good girl," he murmured, leaned in to brush a kiss on her mouth, except Hanny had other ideas. The dog stood between them and stared. "Hanny, don't cockblock."

Kayla giggled—giggled—and figured she was past the point of exhaustion. Bad things had happened—there were people to mourn, like Penny, whose memorial service was in a few days—but she'd survive. She'd continue to. "Did you talk to more FBI agents at the hospital?"

"Too many to count. I'm sure they'll have more questions for you too."

"I have a feeling you won't be the only one with books written about them." She paused. "With all of this, I realized that if none of it had happened, I'd never have met you or Abby. I feel like, I might actually have a real family, finally."

He moved closer and Hanny got off the couch with a grumble and a huff. He pulled Kayla close and murmured, "You do have a real family, baby."

"Good." She hugged him back. "Hey, what's in the bag?"

"Oh, that. Well, the FBI confiscated the camera, so I

figured..." He leaned over and pulled a new camera, still in the box, out of the bag.

"Oh, this is beautiful." She stared at the box, then confessed, "But I don't think I need this anymore."

"Why not?"

"I used to take pictures of pretty things I could've had so I could at least look at them as much as I wanted. But I don't need to take pictures of anything or anyone—especially not of you. Because I get to look at you all the time."

"Day and night," he growled as he pulled her against him. "Try and stop me."

"Only when we're playing," she told him. "Only because I know that turns you on. God, I love you, Teige. More than I thought possible."

His smile was easy. "I probably fell in love with you the first night you took my picture. Maybe that's what pissed me off so badly."

Epilogue

"YOU HAVE NIGHTMARES," Mrs. Mueller said, sitting across from Abby at the kitchen table in Old Man Kennen's house.

Abby's nightmare had been such a fixture in her life, since the night her father was killed at the hands of the Black Magic Killer—she knew the nightmare Willa Mueller was talking about by heart, because it was always the same: *She feels like she can't scream, but she must be screaming inside her head, but her throat's too tight for sound. Her body's heavy, her limbs weighed down like she's been drugged.*

Later, she'll discover it had merely been fear rendering her unable to move or yell. They'll find claw marks in the oak floor, where she'd been digging in with her fingernails, attempting to drag her frozen body across the floor—and toward the scene, not away from it.

Anyone who knows her won't be surprised.

But Abby won't tell Mrs. Mueller all of that, so she simply says, "Yes."

But Mrs. Mueller frowns, holds up a finger while she looks down at the cards and corrects her. "You *had* them. They've stopped.

Abby sat back in surprise, because the woman—or the tarot cards—were both correct. And Abby hadn't even noticed, caught up in healing her injuries, getting stronger and getting the hell out of the hospital. She would've expected the nightmares to get worse post-Mara, or maybe they'd morph into Mara nightmares, but her dreams remained strangely, beautifully calm.

"Calm before the storm," Mrs. Mueller muttered as she flipped another card and stared intently at it.

And that's when Jacoby walked through the door without knocking.

"Fitting," Abby murmured.

Mrs. Mueller caught her eye and smiled, then collected her cards. "We'll do more tomorrow. You've got company."

"Thanks, Mrs. Mueller. This is Jacoby—he's my..." Abby didn't know how to finish that, but Jacoby shook Mrs. Mueller's hand and simply said, "We work together."

"Wonderful. Take care." She winked at Abby as she left and Jacoby just sighed.

"Matchmaker?" he asked.

"Actually, I think she wants to read your tarot cards."

"Yeah, that's what I need—people spying on me. Bad enough you're living with a ghost."

Abby shrugged. "He's friendlier than a lot of the

people I come across at work." She'd rented Old Man Kennen's house once Kayla moved next door with Teige, which happened in a hot minute. It was, it seemed, the perfect solution.

It was a week since she'd gotten out of the hospital and moved her meager belongings there. Although Jacoby had texted her daily to check in on how she was doing, they hadn't really talked at all.

Now, he sat leaned against the kitchen counter. "Hear you're going back to work on Monday."

"I can't sit around here forever. I'm already tired of shopping." She'd lost most of her things in the fire, which was somehow all right. Purifying. She'd been living a transient life with transient things and she'd had nothing in that house she couldn't lose, beyond her life and Kayla's.

Now, she had two couches, a TV and a bed. She was living with two mugs and paper plates. Tomorrow, the clothes she'd ordered would come and she'd wash them and be ready for new cases. Her ribs hurt, her body ached and sleep was still elusive, but the nightmares were gone.

There was something to be said for closure. "Aren't you excited for me to be back?"

He ignored that. "I hear you're thinking about the Academy."

She stared at him. "Either you're psychic or you're just fishing."

He shrugged. "Either way, I'm right."

He was, damn him. "I'm weighing my options. Maybe trying to avoid it all this time was the foolish thing to do."

"Right."

"You think I'm making a mistake, but I can't live for what anyone else thinks."

"So Teige doesn't agree either."

"No, he doesn't. And that's okay," she said stubbornly.

But Jacoby was just as much so. "Don't you get it, Abs? Once you start down this road, it's all over for you. Your life is gone. Don't have kids. Don't get close to anyone. You become as much of a victim of the man or woman you're hunting, maybe more so than any of their other victims. You're the ultimate prize—the trophy. In a way, you're the reason they won't stop—they want to simultaneously horrify and impress you. You're their reason for living—they become obsessed with you too, and what you bring them, whether it's power, notoriety...they think of you as a friend." Jacoby paused. "Serial killers are addicts. So are the agents who hunt them. And you should know that better than anyone."

She stared at him. "I do."

"Then fucking stop it. Right now. Refuse to take on any more cases like this, or I swear to fuck, you'll drown."

"I made Teige..."

"You made Teige do what? Profile? Fall in love? Save a life? He's a big boy. Made his own decision." He paused. "Mara's gone. The obsession dies with her."

He couldn't help but think, *Unless there ends up being a copycat.* Because there always was.

"People know now...the press knows who I am."

It was true—the story spread like wildfire, and granted, it would die down soon enough and leave Abby most of her privacy. Most, not all...and she'd be open to any serial killer looking to make a mark. Several true crime writers had left messages for her at the office, and even though Jacoby had told them all to fuck off, he was pretty sure none of them actually would. "You should quit."

"And do what?" she demanded. "Sit on my ass and write a book?"

"Not a bad idea. Do it under a pseudonym or the crazies will find you." The expression that passed over her face was almost physically painful to him. "I'm sorry, Abby. I know I'm being an asshole about this—"

"Most definitely."

"But I have to remind you about what you're doing. Where you stand...and how much worse things could possibly get."

"For who, Jacoby? You or me?" she challenged.

"Both of us," he admitted. "But I knew I was done for ten years ago."

"So you're leaving, just like that."

"I belong in your past—trust me—it works best like that," he muttered.

"For you or for me?" she challenged.

"Christ, you didn't even want a partner when I arrived," he reminded her.

"Maybe now I do." She took his hand, knowing full well he was never staying. It didn't matter—he would always be in her life, in one way or another. "You saved me."

"You saved yourself—again."

"Kayla helped."

"I guess we'll give her some credit."

"So where will you go now?" she asked.

He shrugged. "I'll see what cases come up."

"What happened to you? Really. I mean, come on, you've seen me at my worst."

"So it's only fair? Bullshit." But he smiled. "It's the boring, clichéd story, Abs. Vic falls for agent. It's inevitable, really. You're spending so much time together. Bonding over anger and fear and pain. They save you and get a hero complex."

"For the record, I don't have a hero complex over you," Abby said dryly.

"Noted."

"Where is she now?"

Jacoby fixed his gaze on her. "Last I heard, he was back at work at the bureau, slowly killing himself."

She frowned, mainly because if the man Jacoby fell for was back at the FBI, that meant Jacoby had been the vic... "There's a lot about you I don't know."

"I'm sure that eventually you won't give a shit."

"I doubt that."

"Think Teige'll be okay?" he asked finally. "I know he's been through hell in his job...and shit like this, almost losing you and Kayla can take a toll after the fact."

He must know from experience. "He's working through it. They both are. Some days are better than others. I guess that's the best all of us can hope for."

"Christ, I hope not," Jacoby muttered. "Hope for more, Abs. You deserve it. All of it."

"So do you."

"Say it enough and maybe one day I'll believe you."

Kayla had moved in with Teige. Of course, Willa Mueller's cards had told her that a while ago, but she always kept things like that to herself. Most people didn't want to know their future.

Teige's sister had taken over renting Old Man Kennen's house. Abby was a pretty woman, pulled between several men, according to Willa's tarot cards. Abby was a sweet girl. But that boy riding the motorcycle... he wasn't for her. No, they both had people out there for them, she mused as she laid the cards out on the table.

Of course, they were also both haunted. And Willa Mueller knew haunted.

Exclusive Previews & More

Sign up for the newsletter of SE Jakes and her alter-ego Stephanie Tyler!

Be among the first to learn not only about new and upcoming books but also appearances and signings as well as special promotions and giveaways!

http://stephanietyler.com/newsletter/

Rule of Thirds

A MIRROR NOVEL (BOOK 2)

Now Available

***Jacoby Razwell has been a grifter, a vic and an
FBI agent in WITSEC...
He's also the brother of a serial killer.***

Jacoby Razwell comes from a family of gypsies, tramps and
thieves...but when he discovers that his sister, Jessica, is a
killer, he immediately tries to extricate himself from her. In
retaliation, his sister leaves him badly scarred, words of
warning carved into his body. He immediately runs to
Special Agent Ward Thayer, the man in charge of the
unsolved murders that Jacoby knows his sister is behind.

Ward takes him in and puts him under the FBI's
protection. But Jacoby wants more, and, after a year of
cooperating with the FBI, he insists on entrance to the
Academy. Jacoby completes the training at Quantico with

flying colors, and soon he's hunting Jessica—and other serial killers—next to Ward. They've become partners at work and partners at home...until Jessica finds a way to tear them apart.

Now, charged with protecting a witness who has his own dangerous secrets to hide, Jacoby and Ward must attempt to bring Jessica to justice at last, all the while knowing that this time they'll have to run toward danger and put their lives—and their relationship—on the line.

Walk in My Shadow
A MIRROR NOVEL (BOOK 3)

Now Available

Danger's never far behind her...

These days, being a US Marshal is easier than it has ever been for Abby Daniels. The demons haunting her from her past have been exorcized on her last job, and while she went through hell, and a serious recovery, she's come out the other end. Her nightmares about almost dying at the hands of a serial killer as a child are gone.

The fact that it took almost dying at the hands of another serial killer just a few months ago is an unfortunate coincidence, but one she doesn't lose much sleep over.

But lurking in the shadows is another dangerous man, tied to someone in her past but wanting to be part of her future...Can she trust him?

Better yet, can she trust herself?

Coming in 2019

And finally...
Don't Miss DOUBLE BLIND: Mirror Book 4...
coming in 2019 from Stephanie Tyler

About the Author

Stephanie Tyler is the *New York Times* bestselling author of romance novels spanning multiple genres, including Romantic Suspense, New Adult, Paranormal Romance and Contemporary Romance. She's a hybrid author who writes for multiple publishers, including Random House, NAL/Penguin, Harlequin, Carina Press, Mammoth Books, Belle Books and Samhain Publishing, as well as Riptide (as SE Jakes) and indie publishing. Her books have been translated into half a dozen languages, nominated for an RT Readers' Choice Award and garnered top picks from *RT Books Magazine* as well as starred reviews from *Publishers Weekly*. She's a frequent workshop presenter and has contributed stories for anthologies for charities, including **SEAL of My Dreams**, which has raised over 150K for the Veterans Medical Association.

Visit Stephanie Tyler at www.stephanietyler.com.

SE Jakes is the pen name for *New York Times* bestselling author Stephanie Tyler, and half the co-writing team of Sydney Croft. First published in 2011, SE Jakes has quickly risen to be a bestselling author in the LGBT romance genre, as well as a fan favorite. Her books are frequently highlighted in *USA Today* and have been reviewed by *Library Journal* and *RT Books Magazine*. She's been nominated by several sites for Favorite M/M author and has finaled in the Goodreads M/M Romance Readers Choice Awards in 7 categories. She's a hybrid author who writes for Riptide Publishing and Samhain Publishing, and she indie publishes as well.

Visit SE Jakes at www.sejakes.com.

Sydney Croft is the alter ego of Stephanie Tyler and Larissa Ione, two *New York Times* bestselling authors who blend their very different writing interests into adventurous tales of erotic paranormal fiction. Together, they developed a world where people with extraordinary abilities, like the power to control storms, could live and work with others like them. The series has been described as "Erotica meets the X-Men," and is unique in its own "erotic superhero romance" niche. Larissa and Stephanie live in different states and communicate almost entirely through email, though they often get together for conferences and book signings.

Visit Sydney Croft at www.sydneycroft.com.

For more information:
www.stephanietyler.com
stephanie@stephanietyler.com

Also by Stephanie Tyler

Mirror Series

Mirror Me

Rule Of Thirds

Walk In My Shadow

Double Blind (forthcoming)

Skulls Creek MC Series

Vipers Run

Vipers Rule

Shelter Series

Shelter Me

Section 8 Series

Surrender

Unbreakable

Fragmented

Defiance Series

Defiance

Redemption

Salvation

The Defiance Series Collection

(Defiance, Redemption & Salvation)

Temperance

Dire Wolves Series

Dire Warning (prequel novella)

Dire Needs

Dire Wants

Dire Desires

Shadow Force Series

Lie With Me

Promises In The Dark

In The Air Tonight

Night Moves

Lonely Is The Night

Hold Series

Hard To Hold

Too Hot To Hold

Hold On Tight

Holding On (novella)

Hot Nights, Dark Desires Anthology

Night Vision (novella)

Harlequin Blaze

Coming Undone

Risking It All

Beyond His Control

Writing as SE Jakes

Men of Honor Series

Bound By Honor

Bound By Law

Ties That Bind

Bound By Danger

Bound For Keeps

Bound To Break

Phoenix, Inc. Series

No Boundaries

Inked Series

Hold The Line

EE LTD. Universe

Free Falling

Hell or High Water Series

Catch A Ghost

Long Time Gone

Daylight Again

Not Fade Away

If I Ever (*forthcoming*)

Dirty Deeds Series

Dirty Deeds

Havoc MC Series

Running Wild

Running Blind

Bluewater Bay (multi-author series)

No Easy Way (novella)

in the *Lights, Camera, Action* Anthology

Writing as Sydney Croft

ACRO Series

Riding The Storm

Unleashing The Storm

Seduced By The Storm

Taming The Fire

Tempting The Fire

Taken By Fire

Three The Hard Way (novella)

Hot Nights, Dark Desires Anthology

Shadow Play (novella)